THE THEORY OF ALL

THE VIRTUOUS TRILOGY FINALE

Written By: Author Y. Deonna

SYNOPSIS

Virtuous has fought and overcome a hard battle that would defeat most, but it is not over. She is trapped between faith and fear. If she chooses love and Theory, then she puts him and his family at risk. If she chooses fear and Greg, then she puts herself at risk. Who should be sacrificed?

Will she choose faith and believe that God will give her hope and a future, or will she allow fear to overcome her spirit?

Theory's world almost ended when he found out he had a son that he never knew existed. As he works to deal with the deception of his ex-girlfriend, his father reappears. It seems like things are getting worse, not better.

Theory loves Virtuous who is everything he prayed for and more, but he hates the thorn that has embedded itself in her. Her father Greg is a problem. He is a problem Theory has had enough of. He knows what to do to solve it, but that would require Vicious, the old him, to resurface. He vowed to never be that person again. He wants to better himself for the woman that he loves, for his family. He must.

Can he? After all the pain, lies and betrayal can he forgive those who trespassed against him, or will he seek vengeance?

Staci and Nocturnal are at a crossroads. They have both done dirt, and their children have suffered for it. Their love was toxic but functional until her lie was revealed.

One lie set off a chain of events that no one could have predicted. Lives will be altered as truths are revealed, some for the better, others for the worse.

Join the crew in this epic finale as they battle between faith and fear, love and loss.

QUOTES

"Affliction is often that thing which prepares an ordinary person for some sort of an extraordinary destiny," -C.S. Lewis
"A woman of virtue attracts a man of value," -Isaiah Borgum

Cover designed by Wicked Smart Designs
Editor: Little Pear Editing Service

This book is a work of fiction. Names, characters, places, and incidents either are products of the author's imagination or are used fictitiously. Any resemblance to actual persons, living or dead, events, or locales is entirely coincidental.

Author Y. Deonna
authorydeonna.wixsite.com/crownedbythecreator

Printed in the United States of America

First Printing: October 2019
Crown Ruby Publishing
ISBN 978-1-7330585-4-4

GET HELP

If you or someone you know is considering suicide, please contact the National Suicide Prevention Lifeline at 1-800-273-TALK (8255), text "help" to the Crisis Text Line at 741-741 or go to suicidepreventionlifeline.org.

CHARACTER TREE

Virtuous→ **Parents**: Big EZ, Valerie (deceased), Valor (twin brother).

Hartford Family→Greg & Addison are Virtuous' legal guardians, their daughter is Maddison, and their son is Jason. Tory is Virtuous' daughter. Cate, Norman, Mamaw LeAnn, Neman.

Theory→Grammy/Naomi, Valor, Maisha, Rika (**Cousins**), **Uncles**: Walker, Baylor, Gerald, Clyde, Luther. **Parents**: Stanley & Angela (deceased). Theory's best friends are Shalamar & Archie. Cordy is Theory's sister.

Nocturnal→ Penelope (sister and Big EZ's wife, mother of Evie & Evan). His best friend was Congo.

Staci→ mother of Chauncory, Sadie and Selma. Jenna is her sister, and Sharifa is Staci's mother.

CHAPTER 1

Shame. Regret. Fear.

Those three emotions pumped through Staci's heart like racehorses. The agony was all-consuming as Staci lay on her bed, unmoving, except for the soft humming of her breath. Dark hair clung to the silk pillowcase like vines; her eyes drifted from one part of the ceiling to the next as her mind repeated her actions. Never in her life had Staci ever contemplated suicide—not until she thought that her death would somehow save her daughter.

Stupid.

Crazy how the mind works, how people think *they* can fix things. That was how she got herself in this position in the first place.

Shame attacked her first. It was as vicious as a black mamba's venom. The frightened look in her mother's eyes and the unasked questions that lingered on her lips were enough to make Staci want to pray for invisibility.

She had decided without prayer or guidance. She leaned on her own understanding and almost made a horrible mistake.

Next, regret. How could she abandon her three children? No, she was not the best mother, but she adored her babies and how dare she take herself away from them? That was an extremely selfish action she was about to commit.

And lastly, fear. Now, she had to face it all. Her pastor had counseled her that facing her lies would not be easy. For some reason, she was cocky enough to think it would not be too bad. However, she underestimated the situation and overestimated how she would react. Her fear was of how Theory and Nocturnal would react toward her and each other. It was a fear she had given into fully.

Unshed tears rested at the brims of her restless eyes. Internal pain ripped through her marrow. When her faith should have been full, it was on fumes.

Not far away, Staci could hear the low hums of her mother's voice but was unable to comprehend her conversation. Then her eyes narrowed in on her sister Jenna. Staci had been avoiding those inquisitive eyes for the past forty-five minutes.

Jenna was sitting in the bedroom, watching her like a hawk. Since Staci's mom was out of the room, Jenna posted up on the chair like a warden who believed that Staci would get another round of the rainbow pills and take them.

That moment of ignorance had passed and would not be revisited again. Staci's time of misery and stupidity were over. She did not want to die. She also did not want her sister looking at her like she was mental. Finally fed up with the scrutiny, she spat, "What Jenna?"

"*What?* How are you asking me that, when you were about to take your life? And for what? Over some dude that looks like *Sid the Science Kid* with a side of Busta Rhymes? There isn't a man on Earth or alien in the galaxy worth dying for and you know that" Jenna admonished, her large brown eyes active with emotion. "I ought to whoop your butt. I mean who does that, sis? Not us. We come from single mothers. We know strength, we know struggle, but we don't attempt suicide. We dig deeper; we fight harder, but we don't ever give up."

Staci was speechless; only her sister would throw in an insult like that while trying to make a point. "Not now, Jenna. Besides, I don't expect you to understand."

Jenna lurched back, offended. "I don't understand?!" Jenna exclaimed, shaking her head. Her animated face let Staci know that Jenna was about to take it up another level. "You have three beautiful children, yet I can't give birth to just one. You were about to make a selfish decision if your mama hadn't come in here. I know it's difficult to see your baby suffering. I can empathize with you not being able to accept her pain, but taking your life that isn't the solution either. How is that even helpful? What would your death have accomplished but more grief? Mm?" Jenna's voice wavered with emotions that nearly caused Staci's chin to quiver. She was doing her best not to do an ugly cry.

"Staci, you got me and your mama, so please never do that again. I told you; stay down here, and I'll help you."

Taking to heart her sister's words, Staci could no longer imprison the tears that now flowed like a waterfall. Everything her sister said was the truth. "I don't know what's wrong with me. Like, I know I was doing stupid stuff when I was younger, but I never considered the consequences. I swear I see it all now that my daughter might die. No matter what any of the pastors or the doctors say, I know it's my fault. We reap what we sow. Sometimes, it doesn't directly impact us but passes on to our children. My daughter suffers because I thought my sins had no consequences. I've cursed her.

So, in my mind, sacrificing my life, dying for my daughter would make God heal her. The jokes on me, though; my sacrifice ain't even worthy," she confessed, teary-eyed.

Jenna leaned back quietly.

"Selfishness has controlled me for a long time. I wanted to show God that even though I've felt worthless my whole life…" she couldn't finish as she wept.

Jenna got up and embraced her. "I keep telling you, Staci, you're not worthless. This idea that you need to die to save your daughter is crazy. That only worked for Jesus dying to save all of us. None are worthy alone; God makes His children worthy," Jenna expressed as she pulled Staci nearer to her.

"I'm sorry that our father's absence made you question your self-worth. Your value isn't in him, or Nocturnal, or even Theory— it's in God! Doesn't the Bible say somewhere that God is the Father to the fatherless?" Jenna's thick eyebrows lifted in question. "You've got to stop picking yourself apart and devaluing yourself. That's easy. I don't know why, but people are quick to see their faults and failures; maybe you should start seeing yourself the way God sees you.

"I don't read the Bible a lot and only go to church because of you, but Staci, if God gave His only Son to die for sinful people, a Son who is perfect and overcame sin and death out of love, then why can't you love yourself? God loves you, even with all your mistakes and sins."

Staci nodded her head in agreement as her sister continued speaking. "Despite your shortcomings, He loves Staci. We're supposed to make mistakes because that is how we learn. We sin because that's our nature without God, but God is the remedy. If a heathen like me knows that much, then surely, you can pray to God to ask Him to let you see yourself the way He does. Stop attacking yourself and start forgiving yourself. If you don't, your children will suffer, and they don't deserve half a mother," Jenna preached.

Chills surged throughout Staci's body. That was the most real advice Jenna had ever given her. Jenna was not saved, but God was using her to speak to Staci.

"Get some sleep; just close your eyes, and I'll hum you a lullaby," Jenna whispered and kissed her forehead.

"I wish I had come down here when you invited me the first time. I would've avoided all this mess. Thank you, sissy."

"Everything happens for a reason. Just sleep, Staci."

A & Ω

Theory was enraged with white-hot anger. No, that was not right; he was completely devastated and disturbed by how Staci kept such a heartbreaking secret from him. *Father.* He was somebody's daddy and never knew.

Staci, after all her betrayal and deceit, robbed him of his son's life for nearly five years. The pain of that reality made him feel unstable. It was like he was bursting out of his skin, yet he was still imprisoned. All he wanted to do was lay his eyes on his son and apologize to him for not being the father he deserved.

Five years felt like an eternity. Five years where his blood, his firstborn, was calling another man daddy and bonding with a man Theory had no respect for. A man who had no code or honor. The level of evil and pure hatred that Staci must have felt for Theory was unimaginable. Still, he had no idea what he ever did to her for her to be so disloyal and disrespectful to him.

How could she make him an absentee father?

During their years together, Theory had never been anything but good to Staci. It was she who cheated. Staci was the one who chose not to support him. Staci chose to leave him. Yet, he would be viewed as the deadbeat father, and he was the one who suffered. It was a punishment he did not deserve.

Rage sizzled underneath his skin, crackling like hot oil in a frying pan. He could feel his body-altering as if he was about to morph into the Incredible Hulk. There was no way in the world God expected him to be calm, cool, and kind; this situation called for Vicious to make an appearance, and once he unleashed that part of him, there would be no coming back.

There was a tiny voice, barely audible, that told him reacting out of anger would do more harm than good.

An overwhelming feeling of deflation and isolation seized his soul. Nothing felt right; it all felt wrong, and nothing anyone said made

6

sense to him. They did not understand. They had not been abandoned, neglected, and abused. Though he survived his parents' stupidity, he never wanted his son to think he was that type of man. This was breaking his heart.

"Theory, just sit down for a moment so that we can talk. I understand your anger. I do, baby, but you must learn to feel emotion, even the difficult ones, and not sin when they become overwhelming. Right now, you look as if you want to destroy somebody, and that won't help this situation," Grammy pleaded.

Theory stopped in mid-step; his dark, rustic eyes glared at his grandmother. The woman who saved him when death surely would have captured him. Grammy was the only mother he'd ever known and would ever have since his own was dead and gone. This woman, who raised him and prayed over him, who fought for his soul; he would have died a million deaths for her and fought the flames of Hell. Now, all he saw was the woman who betrayed him. In his mind, she was just as guilty as Staci and Sharifa. Liars had no place in his life or heart.

Salty tears rested at the brims of his eyes, awaiting his command to fall. Her eyes matched his, except she lost the battle with her tears. They were washing her face. Theory remained unmoved. The agony of her deception refused to let him show her mercy.

"Why didn't you tell me that you suspected Chauncory was my son? Even if you weren't sure, you should've said something to me. How could you betray me, your own blood like that?" His voice was strong and unforgiving. It was a commanding tone that he had never taken with her. He was trembling.

Grammy's sorrowful face softened, like a child who had been scolded. "I wanted to give her the opportunity to do right. I thought she would, Theory. Then I got sick and your father came to town, and there was a whole new set of problems. Everything just happened so fast."

Theory shook his head. It sounded like a convenient excuse to him. "A chance to do right? You had five years to do right and didn't. That's the best excuse you got? Wow! I have got to get out of here. I can't do liars."

"Theo," Valor warned, "Grammy did what she thought was best. Don't disrespect her. She's the only mama we got."

Theory snapped his head toward Valor but didn't speak. Valor could not comprehend this pain. Quivering in fury, Theory turned and marched out the back door. When he returned, he had Logic in his arms, and then he went to his bedroom and started to pack a bag. By the time he was done packing, he could hear his cousins approaching. *Wonderful.*

"Where are you going?" Grammy questioned as if she had the right to know his next move.

Before answering, Theory just glared at her. "Away before I say something or do something I can't come back from. There is no way I'm resting my head in a house where I can't trust the people in it. All you had to do was tell me, but you chose to side with Staci. We all know Staci can't be trusted. Still, you decided to help her conceal her lie, and right now, I can't do you. I love you, Grammy, but I need a moment." Then he looked at Shalamar and Archie. "Let's bounce. I'm going to Anderson to wait for my son."

As he exited the door, his cousins were attempting to enter, apparently frozen by the tension that stole the air from the room, but parted as Theory rushed out. Both girls had perplexed expressions on their faces yet understanding it was best to get out of his way. Theory had nearly left when Valor called out to him, causing him to turn back around.

"Theo, man, you promised."

"I'm not leaving you, Valor, but right now, I'm not in the headspace to be here," Theory answered, though a part of him felt horrible. He and Valor were close, and he promised him that he would never leave him again. This situation required that he take a moment to deal with the weight of everything going on, and he could not do that in the house.

"I'll be back," was all he said before he and his friends headed out the front door.

A & Ω

Virtuous stared at her phone, still in awe of what she heard. Had this man just said that his name was Ezekiel All and that he was her father? How was she supposed to react to that kind of revelation?

"Hello? Are you still there?" the male voice queried on the other end. It was strong and confident, nothing about it sounding street or urban. This man, claiming to be her father, had a calming timbre far different than Greg's often hostile, accusatory tone. And although he

8

was a stranger, he seemed friendlier than the man pretending to be her father now.

"Sir, who are you? I, mean, how did you get my number?" Virtuous asked, her breathing now becoming labored. There had been times when she wished for her biological parents. She had no idea who they were or how they looked, but her heart longed for the safety and comfort that only a parent could bring. Could this be that moment?

"As I stated before, I'm Ezekiel All, your biological father. I don't have long on the phone as I'm currently incarcerated. I just found out that you were alive. I was told that your mother Valerie had aborted you and your brother.

Anyway, I was contacted and told that you and my son are alive, and I wanted to reach out. My attorney, Nadel Wentworth, will be in contact with you. I hope you and Valor will forgive my absence in your life and allow me to see you both. Had I known you were alive; you would have been with me and my family."

Virtuous was speechless, but there were so many questions popping off in her head. *How did he call her without it being a collect call?* "I'm sorry, but I can't talk right now. I'll pass this information along to my brother, and I guess we'll go from there."

"I understand. I know how odd this is, having a man call you out of the blue, claiming to be your father, but I am. I'll respect any decision that you and my son make. I wanted you to know that although I didn't know you and your brother were alive that I love you both. Also, I would love to have a relationship with the two of you. You two also have siblings; their names are Evan and Evie, but they aren't twins," he added, his voice sounded hopeful and welcoming.

"I have one question, and then I have to go. Who contacted you?"

"Addison Hartford."

That caused Virtuous to frown and make her wonder what exactly Addison was doing. "Thank you," Virtuous replied and hung up.

"Vivi, are you okay?" Maisha asked her, but before she could answer, Theory, Shalamar, and Archie flung the front door open, and all three faces were screwed up. Virtuous knew that something was about to go down or something had gone down. They were furious.

"Excuse y'all!" Maisha fussed, rolling her large, mahogany eyes.

"Don't even start with me, Mai; my mind's not in the right place for your mouth today," Theory snapped so hard that even Virtuous was taken aback. Completely forgetting her own issues, her concern immediately turned to Theory.

"Y'all better get out of his way because when he's like this, he ain't listening to nothing and nobody," Rika advised, taking a huge step back and pulling her sister with her.

However, Virtuous was not worried about any of that. Something had upset Theory, and she needed to know what it was.

"Theory, what's wrong?" Virtuous asked, doing her best to keep up with his fast pace. He ignored her and kept walking, so she sped up, got in front of him, and cut off his steps.

It was a bold move that only she could ever try with Theory because she knew he would never hurt her.

"What's wrong? Please tell me," her honeyed voice urgently requested.

It took a moment, but Theory finally recognized her. It was as if his mind had taken him someplace else, dark and far away, and hearing her voice brought him back. That was worrisome.

Theory let out a harsh breath before saying, "Proverbs, please just let me cool off. I don't want to hurt your feelings. I need space."

Virtuous nodded in understanding. "I'll give it to you, but you aren't going anywhere until you tell me what's up. We don't keep stuff from each other," she reminded him, even though she was keeping things from him. However, her situation was different. It could cause Theory more trouble, and that, she would not allow.

Unable to speak again, Virtuous watched as a single tear from each of Theory's eyes roamed down his blushed cheeks. The emotion was so deep that she pulled him into her, completely forgetting about Logic who started to lick her face. Virtuous leaned back and cupped Theory's face. "I'm here; whatever it is, we'll get through it together."

"Staci's son Chauncory is Theo's son, but he just found out, because Sharifa, that's Staci's mom, called and told him. He's hurting because not only did Staci keep that secret for five years, but Grammy knew, too, and no one told him," Archie confessed, his face getting redder as he shared that truth and letting Virtuous know that he, too, was upset.

Virtuous felt her soul leave her body. Whoever said "When it rains, it pours" knew exactly what they were talking about. Sweet heavens, they all needed a break. Shaking her head in sorrow, her heart went out to Theory. No one should ever be denied their child, especially Theory because his greatest fear was to become an absentee dad like his father. "I'm sorry, baby. How can I help?"

It took Theory a moment, but he got himself together. Virtuous could tell that he was struggling with his emotions. As much as she wanted to absorb his pain and hurt, it just was not possible, but she would do what she could.

"I'm going to go get him; just stay here with Grammy and Valor. I know they're both upset with me, but I can't deal with Grammy right now. I don't ever want to disrespect her, but it hurts that she knew something this important and didn't tell me." His tone was even though there were inflections of emotions sprinkled throughout.

Virtuous nodded in understanding. "I can come with you. You're emotional and hurt, but I don't want you going down there and do or say something that you may regret."

Theory offered a slight smile and licked his lips before replying, "I'm good, Proverbs. I won't act a fool. I just want to see my son."

"Understood. I love you. I'm here for you and for your son."

Theory leaned his forehead to hers and inhaled her scent. "Thank you."

"Always and forever, Theory."

"Always and forever," Theory parroted and chastely kissed her lips.

Virtuous let him go, and he packed up his truck. She then turned to Shalamar and Archie. "Keep him safe; if anything happens to my heart, I'm holding y'all responsible."

"That's our boy and we ain't gonna let him get caught up like that," Archie vowed and Shalamar shook his head in agreement.

Virtuous nodded and kissed Theory one more time then watched him leave. It wasn't until she entered Grammy's house that she remembered she and Valor were supposed to celebrate their birthday. How messed up was it that she forgot her own birthday?

They were the big eighteen. This was the first birthday she would share with her twin, and only drama and gloom surrounded what was supposed to be one of the happiest days of their lives. Maybe next year would be better, but at least she had Valor now, and just maybe, their birth father, too.

After greeting everyone Virtuous motioned to Valor so that she could tell him about Ezekiel. It may not be the best time, but he needed to know what was going on. It was possible that this news would get his mind off the Theory/Grammy situation.

Once they sat down, Virtuous told her brother everything.

"So, some man named Ezekiel All called you and said that he's our bio-father and wants to see us?" Valor skeptically questioned his twin.

"Yes. He's an inmate at Tyger River, and he's going to send us the Form 19-127, Request for Visiting Privileges. Until then, we should do an internet search on him and see how he looks and what he got arrested and convicted for. He also told me his attorney was named Nadel Wentworth; maybe we can contact him. I have so many questions, like how didn't he know we were alive if I have his last name? Who signed our birth certificates? Who is our biological mother?"

"Let's get this Theory and Staci situation settled first, and then we can contact this dude."

She nodded in agreement. "Happy birthday, Valor."

He offered her a comforting smile before replying, "Happy birthday, sis. Sorry, our party won't be happening."

CHAPTER 2

"Zeno, you need to come to Atlanta and see about your daughter and granddaughter. You know I would never call you unless it was an emergency. I just stopped Staci from overdosing, and the root of the problem is you. So, do me a favor and be a father for once," Sharifa calmly spoke into the phone.

"What? Why did she do that? That ain't come from my side of the family," Zeno defended.

"She got daddy issues, and it led her to make some serious mistakes that are now coming to light. She's is having a difficult time dealing."

"So, are you saying it's my fault?"

"*I'm saying* you shouldn't have more children than you can care for emotionally. It's not all about money; children need their fathers, and you skipped out. Now, do this one thing, the right thing, for your daughter."

"I'll be there; just text me the address, room numbers, and whatever else I need to know."

"Thank you."

"You're welcome, but you know I'm doing better now, right? I cleaned myself up."

"Good for you, Zeno. Just come see about Staci," she requested and hung up.

"Mama, we need to go to the hospital. Priscilla just called me!" Staci yelled out in a panic.

"Is it Selma?"

"No, it's Nocturnal. He and Congo got into a bad car accident that shut down the interstate. From what Priscilla said, it's not looking good. Please, take me, Mama. I'm mad at him, but I don't want him to die," Staci cried.

It did not take long to arrive at the hospital, and when they did, Staci went right to the information desk to see were Nocturnal was. Just as the lady answered her, Congo's mother was entering with Lourdes.

"Staci, where are they?" Willamina cried, her face flushed and her eyes puffy. Staci's heart broke for her. Congo was her only child.

"In surgery. Come on with me. We can wait together."

"I'll wait, Ms. Willamina," Lourdes called out.

"You don't have to, Lourdes. If you want to be here, stay. I'm not tripping," Staci replied and then reached for her mother's hand and Willamina's as they headed to the surgery floor.

Once they arrived, Staci wanted to leave. Priscilla was crying and fussing. Taking a deep breath, Staci asked the question she needed but did not want to answer. "Is Nocturnal alive?"

"Like you care?" Penelope snapped aggressively, causing Staci to stop short. The accusation was far from the truth. She did care. "This is your fault." She pointed her index finger angrily at Staci.

"Tell it! If my son dies then it's on you," Priscilla added coldly. Her thick lips curled in anger, and her eyes shot daggers. "You out here having another man's child while Nocturnal raising him like he's his own. Then you broke his heart; shame on you and curse your soul if my son dies."

"Don't, Priscilla. Your son ain't innocent and can't spell the word. You don't have the authority to curse anyone's soul. Now, why you throwing stones and speaking curses? Who are your children's fathers? You don't know!" Sharifa fussed. "Staci got enough to deal with, having Selma in NICU. You'll not attack my daughter. I'm saved, but I'm no saint. God is still working the savage out of my soul. Just a reminder that if you come for my daughter then I'll come for you. May God have mercy on you after I'm done!" Sharifa snapped, causing everyone to still.

"Mama—"

Staci was cut off as the doctor entered the waiting room. "Family of Tafi Congo Kabila?"

"That's me. I'm his mother, Willamina Kabila. Is my baby okay?" she asked the gray-haired doctor.

Staci's heart went out to Congo's mother. That look on her face of hope mixed with fear she knew too well. The doctor was about to say something that would either end her world or make it whole again.

Taking unsure steps, Staci drew nearer to Willamina, knowing they shared the same feeling as they both had a child lingering between life and death.

"Follow me, ma'am, so that we can speak privately."

Willamina shook her head violently, and Staci's heart sunk. Quietly, she prayed that Congo was alive. "Tell me what you need to tell me now." Willamina's raspy plea echoed throughout the white, bland walls of the waiting room.

The doctor let out a heavy sigh, and Staci already knew. The answer was in the sorrow of his eyes, and the firm lines that etched the sides of his mouth. "Ma'am, we tried to save your son, but he didn't survive. The internal injuries and bleeding were too severe."

It was like all the air had seeped from the waiting room. It was a tense few moments before Willamina exploded. "Oh, Father in heaven, not my baby! He's all I got! His daddy's dead, and now he is, too." Willamina wept and fell to the floor. "Take me, too, Lord. Take me too. Please don't let me live without my boy."

"Come on, Willamina, let me help you," Sharifa offered, but Willamina tried to fight her off. She was a proud and strong woman, but all Staci saw now was agony and suffering.

"Let me die, Sharifa; just let me die. I got nobody left now. Congo was all I had. God, he was all I had," Willamina lamented as she rocked back and forth as tears drenched her chocolate face. She mumbled in a language that Staci did not understand, but it was clear that her mind had spazzed out.

For a moment, all Staci thought was *God, how could you?* But that was not her place to question or be argumentative with God, though her soul was breaking for a woman who had been nothing but kind to her children. As much as Staci wanted to soothe Willamina, she had no idea what to say.

What can one say to a mother after the loss of her child?

Fear seeped through Staci's entire body. Would Selma or Nocturnal be next? Lord knows she did not want to lose any of them, but Priscilla was right—this death was on her. Had she been honest from the start, this could have been avoided. The burden of guilt hung heavy on her soul.

"Forgive me, Father. One lie, my lie just took a son from his mother, and two lives are still in the balance. God, have mercy. I didn't mean for this to happen." All she thought about was Proverbs chapter 14:12, *There is a way that seems right to a man, But its end is the way of death.* There was so much death attached to her soul and so much blood on her hands that she wondered if she would ever be clean again.

The doctor called for assistance, and all Staci could do was stare. Quickly, her mind flashed back to a mistake she was about to make. This could have been her mother just a while ago had she taken her own life. "Mama, I'm going to the chapel. I need to pray."

Sharifa nodded and went to help Willamina.

"Can I come with you?" Lourdes asked.

"Sure."

The two meandered in silence until Lourdes spoke. "Staci, I apologize for disrespecting you by having a sexual relationship with your man. It was wrong and immature. I had no right to taunt you with it. It was insensitive. I ask for your forgiveness."

"I forgive you. Honestly, I let him do it, you know. A man can only do what you allow and accept. He and I are no longer together, but we'll co-parent our children as best we can."

"He loves you."

"Nocturnal doesn't know what love is. He's comfortable with me. There's a difference. Honestly, all this is on me. I lied. I kept the fact that Chauncory wasn't his son, and now death reigns. If I lose my daughter…"

Lourdes placed a comforting arm around her. "Don't do that, Staci. We don't know each other well, but self-blame isn't the way to get through this. It's not your fault. Like, bad things happen, but that's the time to turn toward God, not put up barriers and belittle yourself."

Never would Staci believe that God would use her enemy to speak to her, but for once, she heard it. First, her sister and now, Lourdes, God was trying to tell her something, and she would listen this time.

A & Ω

Valor put down his game controller when Grammy knocked on the door. Her mood had improved after speaking with him and Virtuous. His sister had left about an hour ago, worried about Theory since he had not called her, but she was doing her best to give him the space that he requested.

"Valor?"

"Yes, ma'am?"

"Your father is here. I thought they were coming tomorrow for church, but he's here now. Just him, not your uncle Stanley or Cordy. Gerald wanted to talk to you if that's okay."

Valor shrugged his shoulders. Honestly, he didn't really know his adoptive father since he spent most of his life being raised by his adoptive grandparents, but he nodded anyway. Maybe Gerald could tell him something about Ezekiel. He always wondered how he and sister got separated.

Grammy nodded and then a second later, Gerald entered. It always amazed Valor how much all Grammy's sons looked alike. Pop had some seriously strong genes because he could not deny any of his sons.

"Hey, Val." Gerald's deep voice echoed in the quietness of the room.

"Hey."

"May I sit down?" Valor could tell that Gerald was nervous. He made eye contact, but there was uncertainty in his demeanor, and he kept rubbing his hands up and down his pants leg. A sign of his nervousness, Valor concluded.

"Yes, sir."

Gerald offered an unsure smile but took a seat on the recliner. "Happy birthday," he replied and handed Valor a gift. He took the envelope and opened it. There were tickets to a Carolina Panther's game. Showing no emotions, Valor kept his eyes on Gerald.

Taking the silence as a cue to say something, Gerald took a deep breath and spoke. "I'm sorry about my absence in your life. I don't expect tickets to see your favorite football team to right any of my wrongs." He nervously licked his lips and rubbed his hands together, "It took me a long time to get to a place where I was comfortable being around people and assimilate into civilian life. When I came back home from the military and found out what your mama was doing and how you weren't being treated well, it broke me. I lost the last bit of humanity in me.

I was kind of scared that I might hurt you in my unstable mindset. So, I did the only thing I knew to do. I brought you to my parents. It was a decision that I struggled with; however, I saw myself going down the same path as Stanley, and I'd die before I attempted to offer you as payment for an addiction." He exhaled slowly before continuing. "I went to Veteran Affairs and got some help. It took a while, but I was getting myself together. During that time, your mother left me, and we got a divorce. I don't know where she is or even if she's alive. She kind of just disappeared. I always assumed she ran off with her lover.

Anyway, I found Stanley and we made our way to the coast and settled down in New Orleans. I was too much of a coward to reach out to you, even after my father died. I felt like such a failure. My parents didn't raise a failure, but I kept believing that was all I was. I didn't want to face you; I was a coward for that. But I followed your career. You're a phenomenal young man. Ma told me that the Naval Academy is recruiting you heavy. I just wanted to tell you that I'm proud of the man you're becoming. I pray daily for you.

The last thing I wanted to say is that I love you, Valor. After my last tour, I was in a bad headspace. Killing was what I was trained to do, but death takes a toll; seeing your friends die eats away at your soul. In all that I suffered, I never stopped loving you. You were and will always be my motivation. I know I don't have the right, but do you think you'll ever be able to forgive me?"

Valor took a deep breath. Gerald was being sincere, and he knew that it took a lot to come and face his son and admit being a failure and a coward. "You were sick. I don't fault you for that. I don't think you're a failure or a coward. I, mean, you served your country bravely. You're a decorated soldier, and that's not something a lot of people can claim. In my short time on this earth, it seems, to me, the people hardest on themselves are themselves. They become their own worst enemies.

Pop and Grammy wanted you and Uncle Stanley home. They were willing to do whatever to make our family whole again. I'm not mad. I can't see the worth in being angry with someone like that. I thought it was something wrong with me. I thought I made you and Ma leave, just like my bio-parents, but Theory and I talked about it and that helped. I prayed about it. I forgive you. Holding onto grudges only hurts the person that's holding them, and I'm too young to be that bitter. This handsome face wasn't made to wrinkle," he joked.

At that, Gerald started to laugh and cry. "You're an amazing and handsome young man. I wish I had that kind of wisdom at your age. Can I hug you?"

"Yeah, Dad, you can hug me," Valor replied, getting up and meeting him in the middle of his bedroom.

Gerald pulled him into a deep embrace, and Valor let him. It was apparent to him that his dad was hurting and needed to share his story.

"Will you say it again? Just call me Dad one more time. Lord knows, I missed that word," he requested tearfully.

"Forgive yourself, Dad. I honestly hold no anger against you."

"I love you, son. I'm so sorry I missed so much of your life. I'm here now if you'll accept me. I'm prepared to move here or do whatever you need. I just don't want any more separation."

"I love you, too."

Gerald chuckled and pulled back. "I left you a little boy, and I return to find you a young man. You're special, Valor. So special."

"Thanks."

"Where's your sister? She met me and Stanley in the hospital and told us we better not mess up, or we were going to deal with her."

"You met, Virtuous?" he asked with a smile. His sister was a fierce little something. He loved how she watched out for him and Theory. "Actually, she just left about an hour ago. Believe it or not, we just reunited. It was all God's plan, I believe. You got some time; we can talk about everything."

"I have all the time in the world for you, son. I owe you a lifetime of apologies."

"Let that go. I'm not holding onto the past; you're here now. There's a lot going on, so we can't linger on what we can't change."

"Amen." Then Gerald smiled. "I got my boy back," he gushed like a child and pulled Valor into another embrace.

CHAPTER 3

Theory decided that waiting in Anderson for Staci and his son was not going to cut it. He was too antsy waiting, and needed to do something with is nervous energy. So, he and Archie decided to drive to Atlanta. Yulonda shared that Nocturnal and gotten into a car accident and was in a coma. Congo was in the car, too, and had not survived. Even though Theory was upset with Staci, he hated that she was dealing with both her daughter's premature birth and the possibility of losing her daughter's father. He did not wish that kind of burden on anyone. However, he needed to meet his son.

"You good, bruh?" Archie inquired as they arrived at the apartment complex that Sharifa texted him to pick up Chauncory.

"Man, I was angry then irritated and now, I'm nervous. What if my son hates me? Like, what if he's like *You ain't my daddy?* That would kill me," Theory confessed.

"He won't. Dude, you're like the kid magnet. Cutie met you for the first time and was instantly your best friend. Think how much more it'll be with your son."

Theory hoped so. Taking another deep breath, he and Archie exited the truck at the same time and headed to the apartment that housed his son.

"Theo, are you going to knock, or are we just going to stand here?" Archie chortled.

Theory nodded and knocked on the door. It was opened immediately as if his presence was already known. On the other side stood Jenna, whom Theory had not seen in years. Still, he recognized her by because of her unique choice of dress. Her clothing and hair were always as colorful as her mouth. It looked like she took a bath in a box of Crayola crayons.

"Come in Vic- I, mean, Theory. My sister told me you don't like to be called by your street name no more; so sorry about that. Chauncory is in the back room. He knows you're coming, and I showed him some old pictures. Staci still had two from when you were a kid, and when

Chauncory looked at the little boy in the pictures, he thought it was him." Jenna dropped her head for a moment as if she were searching for the right words. Her hands slid up and down her thighs before she spoke again.

"Look, I'm sorry about what my sister did, and when she's stronger, I know she'll come to you like a woman and personally apologize. Right now, she's overly emotional. She even tried to take her life. I, mean, it's been that kind of week.

Anyway, I've packed Chauncory's stuff and wrote down his clothing and shoe sizes, likes and dislikes. He has allergies, but they aren't severe. Y'all are welcome to stay the night and leave in the morning if you'd like. Just lock up if you stay. Staci told me to tell you that the lawyer will call you and that she won't fight you on visitation or anything like that. She's going to stay here. I only have one request: please don't punish my sister and take Chauncory away from her for good. I, mean, you have a right too, but…"

"Just let me see my son."

Jenna nodded. "Chauncory, c'mere, baby. Your Daddy and Uncle Archie are here to see you."

Theory kept his eyes fixated on the hallway until his mini-me arrived. His heart stopped beating, and Archie exhaled loudly as if the wind had been knocked out of him. It took them both a moment to recover.

"Yo, that's your boy," Archie stated, eyeing the child in bewilderment. "Dude, that's you. Lil' dude looks just like you as a kid. Man, how we never noticed before now is beyond me."

Theory got down on one knee and waited for his son to approach him. He did not want to scare him or make him feel uncomfortable as emotions flooded him. Without realizing it, tears slid down his face in rivulets. He didn't even feel them. He only became aware of them when Chauncory lifted his small hands and wiped them away.

"Are you sad?" he asked. A flummoxed expression covered his youthful face.

"No. I'm happy. These are happy tears."

Chauncory nodded. "You look like me."

Theory chuckled. "Yeah, the Campbell genes are dominant."

Theory paused for a moment and then asked, "Can I hug you?"

Chauncory nodded yes, and Theory pulled him into an embrace. "I love you."

"Mommy said you did. She said that you're a good daddy and that I'm going to stay with you and meet my other family."

"That's right. Are you hungry?"

"Yes, sir."

Theory chuckled; his son had manners and was well-spoken. "Cool. Let's get something to eat. We can take your auntie and sister, too."

"Okay, Daddy."

Theory's heart burst into a million pieces. He was too weak to get back up. His son had accepted him and called him "Daddy". He pulled him into another hug. At least Staci had done a good job of preparing their son to meet him.

Theory felt Archie's hand on his back, and he was thankful for the support. He could also hear Jenna crying.

"Theo, if you don't mind, I'd like to pray over you and your son," Archie offered.

They bowed their heads and delivered a prayer of thanks, protection, and forgiveness.

A & Ω

Virtuous finally arrived at her grandparents' home, her mind on Theory and his finding out about his son. She prayed that everything would work out well, that his son would welcome him with open arms. The other issue that plagued her mind was the possibility of having a father and what that finally meant.

Valor warned her about becoming too invested because it could be that the man was not their father, or that they might not like what they found out about him. However, in Virtuous's mind, that was easy for her brother to say because he had another father, but she had never known the feeling. She never considered Greg a father because of the horrific things he did to her and the rest of the family.

Opening the car door, she quickly exited and shook her thoughts. Her mind needed to be on the girls and how she was going to save them and herself, too. November was quickly approaching, which meant December, the month that she was supposed to return to Greg, was fast approaching. Her stomach soured at the idea of being back in his clutches.

Mumbling to herself, Virtuous jogged up the steps and halted on the porch as Mamaw came shooting out the door holding the cordless V-

Tech phone. Her face was ashen; her eyes wide, turning red as she fought back relentless tears.

"What's wrong, Mamaw?" Her heart skipped in anticipation of her grandmother's reply.

"Honey, there was an accident while the men were hunting in Utah. Greg was shot twice."

"Is he dead?" God forgive her for even wanting that to be a possibility, but if he were, she would finally be safe.

"No, thank God. Neman and Norman have taken him to the hospital. Do you think you and the girls will be okay if I fly out to Utah tonight? They said they don't need me, but that's my baby boy, and I need to be there."

"Yes, ma'am, we'll be fine, and I'll take care of the store and the farm. Don't worry about anything. Please keep me updated," Virtuous nearly gushed.

"Cate will still be at home, so she can help you."

"Don't worry, Mamaw. Do what you need to do. I'll help you get packed."

It didn't take them long, and Mamaw was out the door, headed to get on the first plane leaving. Cate drove her, and as soon as they were gone, Virtuous called Tamari and told her what happened.

"You know what, Vivi? God don't like ugly. Greg's reaping. He needs to take this time to repent and reset," Tamari fussed, sounding like one of the mothers of the congregation that sat on the first pew in Theory's church.

"When Mamaw told me he was shot, I almost started to Milly Rock," she laughed. It felt so good to laugh after so much sadness and heartbreak.

"Girl, you're crazy." There was a pause for a moment, but Virtuous had a feeling that Tamari had more to say. It was in the way her breathing was interrupted.

"Just say it, Tamari."

"Um, do you think you're ready to tell someone? I, mean, other than me about the abuse? Maybe we can tell your art teacher, Mrs. Valmont? She'll believe you. This would be the best time while he's out of commission. I would say tell my daddy, but he's out there with them."

Virtuous bit her bottom lip, thinking about what to do. She had never thought about telling Mrs. Valmont. Her art teacher adored her, and besides Serena was probably the only other woman she was close with. But how could she start that conversation?

"I'll think about it. Listen, let me call you back. Tory is up, and she's whining."

"Okay. Hey, I can come over. In fact, I'm sure my mom would let me stay over since you are home alone."

"Well, ask her, I'd love the company. A lot has gone down today, and I need my bestie."

"I'm coming over. I'll pack a bag, so I can stay awhile."

CHAPTER 4

It was late when Theory, Chauncory, and Archie arrived at church. They had missed Sunday school but managed to make it to service. It was not until Theory called Virtuous to apologize for his actions and ruining her party that he remembered that he was supposed to sing a solo.

Virtuous was not even upset with him over not celebrating her special day. She said she got the best gift by knowing that he was reunited with his son. For that, Theory was beyond thankful. He had the best woman any man could ever pray for. Virtuous was rare and he would never do anything to intentionally jeopardize their relationship.

As they headed to the family pew, Theory's feet halted; there were extra people than usual. Uncle Gerald was sitting by Valor, and he assumed the little girl was his sister. She was holding hands with Cutie and on Virtuous' lap was Tory. Additionally, Jason and Tamari were present, as were Yulonda and Shalamar, but what gave him true pause was Stanley.

Quietly, Theory grabbed his son and sat down on the pew. When Virtuous noticed him, she was about to get up and sit beside him, but he shook his head no. There was no reason to uproot everyone. Besides, he would be getting up soon to sing. No sooner than he had the thought did the minister of music wave for him to prepare for his solo.

"Chauncory, I have to sing now, but I'll be right back. You just hang out with Uncle Archie."

"I want to sing, Daddy."

"Alright, come with me."

Chauncory nodded and Theory nodded to Virtuous and winked at her. She gave him a beautiful smile that had his heart beating double-time.

"Daddy, who is that? She's pretty!" Chauncory exclaimed loudly, pointing at Virtuous and making everyone laugh, but Virtuous was blushing furiously.

"That's your future stepmom," Theory whispered in his ear.

Chauncory turned around, eyes the same as Theory's. Shoot, he even had Theory's soft curls. Every time Theory looked at him, he was in awe. He did not even sleep last night because he was just in reverence of his son. "That's you?" Chauncory asked, his small eyebrows lifting in surprise.

Archie bent over laughing, and it was funny because Chauncory was nothing but proper. The way his son spoke with such clarity reminded him of how Valor was as a child. However, what he just said, clearly sounded like something Archie would say. Archie was already rubbing off on his son.

"Boy, c'mon here! Yeah, that's me," he teasingly scolded, placing a gentle hand on top of his head.

Chauncory smiled hard and waved at Virtuous before they made their way to the choir stand and Theory made the introductions.

"Good morning, everybody. Archie and I apologize for arriving late, but I just found out yesterday that this little, handsome dude is my son. We weren't going to come because I didn't want to overwhelm him, but he said, '*Daddy, it's Sunday; we need to be at church.*' So, here we are. He also just told me he wanted to sing a song, so if y'all don't mind, I'll let him sing instead of me.

"Let that baby sing!" the congregation called out.

Theory pulled the microphone down to Chauncory's height and then asked, "What song do you want to sing?"

"I'm just five, so I don't know a whole lot of songs." That made everybody laugh. "Today, I'd like to sing *O Happy Day.*"

Theory smiled. "Sing when you're ready," Theory told him, having no idea if his son knew all the words. He was prepared to help, but surprisingly, his son didn't need any help.

Chauncory may have only been five, but he sang that song like a grown man. He took the microphone off the stand and started walking and singing. Not only did his son look just like his daddy, but he could sing like him, too. Chauncory had everyone on their feet, singing along with him, and all Theory could do was smile like a proud father. Tears just fell from his eyes.

Oh happy day (oh happy day)
Oh happy day (oh happy day)
When Jesus washed (when Jesus washed)

When Jesus washed (when Jesus washed)
When Jesus washed (when Jesus washed)
He washed my sins away (oh happy day)
Oh happy day (oh happy day)

Theory looked over the congregation, and his eyes fell on Stanley. Not for the first time did he wonder how his father could abandon him. Theory would fight Hell's inferno to save his son, and his father used him as currency for drugs. *Weak.* Stanley Campbell was a weak, worthless, reckless human being. Only that kind of person could do what he did.

Theory quickly closed his eyes and whispered a prayer of peace. *Not today, Satan.* Today and every day he would celebrate his son and being a better father than the one he was given.

"Amen," Apostle Amos hummed from the pulpit, causing Theory's eyes to snap open.

"That's what I love to see—our children praising God. We'll have one more selection, and then I'll share the message."

After that, Theory and Chauncory sat back down. Theory's heart was overflowing. Just yesterday, he was a broken man, and today, he was wholly mended. He adored his son and couldn't help but begin to shout. The spirit was in him, and he could not deny what the Lord had done and was doing for his life.

Today's message hit home for Theory. Apostle Amos challenged the congregation to reset their mental thoughts from a savage state of mind to a saint state of mind. Theory knew that he lingered between the two, and as Apostle Amos said, that was the same as being lukewarm—either you're a soldier for Christ or a savage for the world. That had Theory thinking, but that was what he liked about Apostle Amos; he did not sugarcoat the message.

"Theory."

Theory looked up and saw Deacon Hayes. Church was over now, and most people were talking or shaking hands while Theory was lost in thought. "Yes?"

"If you have a moment, Amos and I would like to talk to you."

Theory frowned, not in anger, just in confusion. He and Deacon Hayes met at least once a week, so he was concerned as to why they needed to meet now. "Right now?"

27

"Well, Naomi invited us over to the house to celebrate Virtuous and Valor's birthday. She also told me about your birth father and the situation with your son. I just wanted to counsel you."

Theory nodded. That was why. He needed all the help he could get, but he still was not ready to interact with Stanley, though he did want to meet his sister. He had been watching her throughout the services, and she was too precious. Strangely, she favored their mother Angela in almost every way. There was nothing "Campbell" about her. The only trait she and Theory shared was their soft, curly hair.

"That'll work."

A & Ω

"DJ Trek is in the house! I just want to wish the twins Valor and Virtuous a blessed and prosperous, epic eighteenth birthday. Let's thank God for bringing Virtuous to us. She's a great addition to the family and is an honorary Campbell. Big shout out to Uncle Gerald and Uncle Stanley; we're glad y'all home. Oh, and shout out to Cordy, the cutest Campbell ever! Now, I'm 'bout to hit y'all with that *Family Reunion* by the original O'Jays."

"Whatchu know about that?" Uncle Gerald called out.

"Unc, I'm *that deejay.* I know all the music," he teased then two-stepped.

Virtuous giggled at Trek's antics. Trek was a cool and fun guy. His special talent was smoothing out the awkwardness of any situation.

Virtuous then turned her attention to watching the children play. She was sitting at the table with Tamari, Rika, and Maisha. Tamari had just finished telling Virtuous that her father had passed his Lieutenant's exam. When she came over to spend the night, they did not talk about anything but just watched movies and ate Quinn popcorn. Later that night, Mamaw called, advising that she made it safely and that Greg was going to be okay.

"Tamari, I still can't believe your father knows Grammy."

"I know. It's a small world, but he went to school with some of her sons."

Virtuous nodded and their conversation died down as Valor padded over and handed Tory over to Virtuous. "I'm coming back to get her. I have to take care of something."

Virtuous frowned but Valor reassured her that everything was okay. Still, that did not make her feel any better. There was tension between the other four brothers and Gerald and Stanley. It had been like that, even in church. It was obvious the brothers felt, like Theory. They felt that Gerald and Stanley, mainly Stanley, no longer had a place in the family. Stanley had hurt them all, first with his treatment of Theory and then by not coming to his father's funeral.

Virtuous noticed that neither Stanley nor Theory were around, and she wondered if that was what Valor went to check on. Instead of inquiring, Virtuous nodded to her brother, pulled Tory into her, and tuned into the current conversation.

"Whatever happened to those other girls? You know, the ones with blue and purple hair?" Tamari asked Rika.

"I forgot about them. Nora Jean was the one after Theory. I'm not feeling them. I hope they don't show up," Virtuous answered honestly.

Maisha burst into laughter. "Tell it, Vivi! Don't nobody come for Theory." she teased.

"Right!"

"Oh, you mean Deandrea and Celina? Girl, they fell off, along with Nora, but Celina called me and gave some tea," Rika replied.

"What?" Tamari questioned leaning over in her seat, and Virtuous shook her head. She did her best to not play into gossip, but honestly, she was curious, too.

"Well, just like Theory said Nora is about that money and material power. So, she was messing with Congo, but I don't think it was serious. She was also messing with Nocturnal. Now, wait for it—she's pregnant."

"What?" everybody chorused at once.

Rika put her hands up. "Yes, you heard me correctly, and it's Congo's child because she was pregnant before she started messing with Nocturnal. Now, who pregnant without a ring or a degree? She came for Staci, and now she's eating her own words. It's sad that Congo is dead and don't even know he has a child on the way," Rika replied sadly.

"My goodness. That hurts my heart," Virtuous replied, her hand over her heart.

Then she looked over at Rika. "How are you feeling? I know that Congo meant something to you."

Rika shrugged. "I'm sad that he died, like that really hurts, but he wasn't mine. You know, I liked him, but he wasn't into me like that.

Theory was right. I was out of my depth. I just want a good guy. And Nimo, he's more my speed."

"Yeah, Nimo is a good guy, and I'm glad you two are talking," Virtuous agreed.

"Me too," Maisha added. "I hate how Ms. Willamina must be feeling now. No parent wants to bury their child, and he was her only child. Mama said we can go visit her. I wonder if she knows about Nora Jean being pregnant. Maybe I should call and check in on Nora Jean."

"It's just so much. Theory finding out that Chauncory is his son, and now Congo's death and Nocturnal lingering in the balance. I'm upset with how Staci handled the issue, but I feel so sorry for her as well. Then I look at Theory." She paused for a moment. "I'm just, like, God, I know you need to break us to remake us, but *my heart* has been through it," Virtuous continued.

"He's strong, though, and he has us," Rika added.

"He is, but even strong people need breaks and support. I refuse to let any of this break him down."

"I'm glad he has you, Vivi. You make him better. He's focused on the right things now. Prior to meeting you, he would have probably lost his mind. Did you see how proud he was when Chauncory started singing? Oh, my goodness, I was in tears. Like, I felt that love. Theory has more challenges to come, but he knows Christ is the answer," Maisha assured her.

They all nodded.

"Mai, come dance with me," Jason called out as he sauntered over to the table.

Virtuous watched the smile on both of their faces, and it warmed her. Jason needed this kind of normal, and he deserved to be loved. Mai was good for him. Greg had taken a lot from them, but slowly, their broken pieces were being reassembled to be stronger than they were before.

"Aye, Tamari, this my song; come and dance with me," Shalamar requested.

That was surprising because Shalamar was just a cool and quiet dude. He did not give off "dancer" vibes. He was always the thinker in the group. Virtuous knew that he was going to be a fantastic social worker. He told her that he wanted to get his MSW and DSW. The boy was smart enough to do it, too.

Virtuous sat back and a warm feeling overcame her. Her time would come soon; somehow, all this madness would end.

"Will you play with us?" Chauncory asked, looking so much like his daddy that Virtuous wondered how Staci kept the secret for so long.

Virtuous just could not get over how much he looked like Theory. "Sure, sweetie."

CHAPTER 5

Theory sat quietly in his bedroom, wanting to be anyplace else but here. Besides, the bedroom felt extremely cramped with Deacon Hayes, Apostle Amos, and Stanley inside. This was a bad idea. There was nothing good that would come from this assembly.

Theory's arms were crossed defensively as he was in no mood to have any conversation with Stanley. Just because Valor forgave Gerald and they were rebuilding their relationship did not mean that was going to happen with Theory and Stanley. Their situation was entirely different.

"Well, I guess I'll start," Deacon Hayes' velvety voice cut through the thick silence that was nearly suffocating.

"There's nothing to say, Deacon Hayes. You're my mentor, and I appreciate and respect your godly wisdom. However, I'm not in the right frame of mind to deal with him. I probably never will be. All I want to do is have a relationship with my sister and be a great father to my son. On that, I don't need direction. I've been a big brother to Val, and Pop, God rest his soul, taught me about being a father. Plus, I have a boatload of uncles. So, I don't need that man," Theory emphasized by pointing his index finger at Stanley, "in my life. His presence is equal to that of Satan's because all he knows how to do is seek and destroy. I'm not here for it," Theory snapped and then rose his seat.

"Now, hold on, Theo, hold on," Amos interjected. "I don't know the full extent of your father's betrayal, but he and I spoke before we came in here, and he just wants to talk to you, Theo. No matter what, he's your father, and our Father tells us to '*Honor your father and your mother, so that you may live long in the land the Lord your God is giving you*' (Exodus 20:12)."

Theory looked up at Amos, a man he respected as much as Deacon Hayes, but neither of them was going to tell him how to feel. "Exactly. You don't know. To your point, my grandparents raised me, and I did and do honor them. Also, the Bible states '*Fathers, do not provoke your children, lest they become discouraged*' (Colossians 3:21) and

'*And you, fathers, do not provoke your children to wrath, but bring them up in the training and admonition of the Lord' (Ephesians 6:4).* The keyword in those verses to me is '*Do not provoke'.* Well, his very presence is provoking. He sold me; he and his wife sold me for a baggy of death and destruction. They abused and neglected me."

The anger, the emotions, the feeling of being that scared little boy attacked his senses as if it happened yesterday. His own parents sold him for a temporary high, and that was what these people did not understand. A whisper of a tear tickled his left eye, but it evaporated as quickly as it appeared.

Theory took a deep breath and continued. "You know how I survived before Grammy and Pop took me in? I bathed in and drink rainwater. I ate whatever was around, stale and outdated food, or food their junkie friends would throw in the trash. Sometimes, their dealer took mercy on me and got me a Happy Meal. How does your dealer care more about your son than the people who created him? Mm? Tell me that!

We had mice, roaches and bed bugs, and it was by God's grace that I didn't die from an infection. So, no, I'll never honor him. He is no father, and he is no man. What is there to honor? A memory? A fictional father? He failed me left and right. I owe him nothing." Theory finished strong; his voice was even with no show of emotion. The weakness he nearly showed prior was replaced with cold fury.

"I get it, son. You hate me, but—"

Theory let out a cutting laugh, halting Stanley's response. "That's a bold and incorrect assumption. You don't get it! I told you about calling me '*son'.* That's the most disrespectful word to leave your lips. I don't belong to you! Let's get that clear now. Secondly, I don't hate you; to hate you would require that I feel something for you, that we're connected by some invisible thread. I feel nothing for you. You stopped existing to me a long time ago. I buried you long before I paid my last respects to Pop, *my real father.* So, don't do me. Don't tell me anything because when it comes to Theory Correion Campbell, *father* of Thesis Chauncory *Campbell,* you don't know nothing. Let's keep it that way." Then he looked over at Amos and Deacon Hayes. "Thanks, but you all should go and enjoy the celebration. I know I am. I'm done with this," Theory stated calmly and got up from the chair, fixing his clothing as he sauntered off out his bedroom, leaving the rest of them there with blank expressions.

"Theory, at least let me tell you about Angela, about her family, your sister," Stanley called out, causing Theory to stop mid-stride, turn around, and march back to his bedroom.

"Dude, Angela is dead. Grammy told me that already. I can't mourn a woman I never knew. As for my sister, I'm about to talk to her now."

Stanley looked defeated. "Just sit down, please. This conversation won't be about us, just your sister and your mother," he offered.

Theory just glared at him. "Give him that much, for me, Theo," Deacon Hayes implored.

Out of respect, Theory nodded but stayed posted up on the door. He was not moving. "I'm listening."

"We can leave," Amos offered.

"No, stay. Deacon Hayes is Theory's mentor, and you're his pastor. You should both stay."

They nodded, and Stanley continued. "Well, your mother died during childbirth. There were some serious complications. She had been advised not to get pregnant. You know, Angela was always stubborn. She wanted another child, a chance to get right what she messed up with you. It took her time, but she got clean then she went back to drugs because when she got clean, she had to face what we did to you. She left me. I don't know where she wandered to.

"Eventually, she found her way back to me, and she was pregnant. So, Cordelia Rose isn't my biological daughter, but I was there for everything. I signed her birth certificate. During the time Angela was away from me, she reconciled with her family back in North Carolina. They got some money. Her father ran for governor of North Carolina. He's currently a US congressman. He doesn't care much for me. He blames the downfall of his daughter on me, and I understand that. Anyway, they want to meet you. When you were born, they created a trust fund for you. I think you get it in your late twenties or at least a percentage of it."

Theory leaned over, laughing hysterically, causing everyone in the room to go silent. They probably thought he had lost his mind, but this was too much. "Yo, I knew it was something. Do you want the money? I mean 'cause I've been asking myself why you'd pop up like this. It can't be because you feel sorry or because you care. I, mean, why is this ghost haunting me? I see it now. You see dollar signs. Ole grimy money vulture, that's all you are. I have no idea how much it is but take it. Then I never want to see you again. Oh, and leave Cordy. I can't let you mess up her life like you were determined to end mine."

Stanley's eyes widened at the accusation, and he leaped out of his chair and lunged for Theory, who did not even blink or react. He just glared at Stanley as Amos held him back.

"Back up off my brother," Valor interjected, prepared to defend Theory, not that he needed it. Theory had no idea where Valor came from or how long he had been present, but he, too, was in beast mode. Theory tapped him, letting him know it was all good.

"I won't let you keep disrespecting me like that. I hurt you. I know I did. I hurt your mama. I accept that, but all I've ever done is love, Cordy. My blood doesn't flow through her veins, but that's my daughter, my salvation. All I did wrong with you: I'm doing right by her." Seeing that Theory remained unresponsive, Stanley's body started to shake, and he broke down.

"Why can't you just let me love you, Theory? Why you want to punish me. You want me to feel the agony that you felt? I feel it, Theory." Stanley cried placing his hand over his heart. "I damaged an innocent little boy. Down deep in my soul I feel that daily. I can't get right because of it. I don't want money from you. I just want to make better memories with you and with my grandson," he wept. He was down on his knees, and Theory just stared at him, unyielding. He truly deserved a BET Movie Award for his performance.

"One, two, three…six, seven, eight…twelve, thirteen, fourteen…" Theory continued until he got to twenty-one. "Twenty-one years, Stanley. Twenty-one years of your absence, but your treatment of me seeped through my pores, wove through my flesh, corroded the goodness, and left nothing but embers for a strong wind to blow away." His flat hands fisted as he expressed his hurt and pain.

"Twenty-one years of feeling like I was floating in the air, loveless, homeless, confused, angry, violent, and full of hate. I was *vicious*. Twenty-one years of looking into a mirror and seeing nothing, questioning my worth, wondering why my dad didn't want me. Twenty-one years!" Theory shouted, punching the wall. Valor pulled him back to keep him calm.

"I was out here in the streets looking for what you refused to give me. I was looking for acceptance, love, for someone to tell me I was worthy; that I belonged. That I was born for a purpose, that my life was more than what you did to me.

I should have gotten that from you and Angela, but that pipe and them little white lines were all y'all cared about. You stole my innocence, my confidence, and nearly, my life. I never did anything to you for you to throw me away like you did. *Nothing!* I got locked up looking for what you stole and shattered. That's why you can't love me, dude.

"When you had the chance, you blew it. After Pop died, you should have come back. You should have said *sorry;* you should've said *I love you, Theory, and I'll give my life to make it right,* but like the worthless, weak, coward you are, you didn't. Don't you bring that sappy fake tear-jerking, I-love-you-boohoo to me. You don't exist, ashes-to-ashes and dust to deadbeat dads. I don't need you, and I don't want you. Eat that old man. You need to see what it feels like to be abandoned, to have your virtue stolen, to question your value, your very existence. Live in that realm for a while," Theory fumed before taking a deep cleansing breath. He was about to walk away, but he had something else to say.

"You know what? I still got the victory, though. You gave me nothing, but God gave me everything. I got a girl that loves me despite how you and Angela broke me. Her eyes light up like the sunrise when I enter a room. She calls me her heart. All that ugliness and poison y'all poured into me, she cured. I mean something to her; she *wants* me. She accepts me and my son and asks for nothing in return. That's love, but you don't know about that."

Theory let out an annoyed chuckle before continuing. "I got a son that loves me, even though I didn't know he existed until yesterday. I'd die for my son, *my son.*" He patted his chest to show emphasis. "There is nothing I wouldn't sacrifice for him, and we only been together twenty-one hours. You had twenty-one years and ain't did nothing but piss me off. Get up and get out. I'm tired of seeing this show, and I'm tired of you. My sister will always be welcomed, in my home, and my heart, but not you. I can't deal with a liar, a user, and an abuser," Theory snarled.

"I'm sorry, Theory. God knows I'm so sorry. If I could redo my life then I would. Forgive me! I hear you, and I'm here now for you."

Every man in that room was in tears. Amos had turned completely red, tears falling just as hard and constant as Theory's. Even Deacon Hayes was sniffling. Theory stood unmoved, even as the tears poured violently from his eyes, staining his shirt as they mixed with his running nose. He was unaffected by Stanley's plea.

"Don't you dare ask me for something you never offered. Your presence is unwanted. Leave."

At that, Theory saw a bit of life seep from Stanley. The air in the room had shifted, and everyone felt it.

"Valor, take Theo outside; let him calm down," Deacon Hayes requested.

Valor nodded and pulled Theory outside where a few of their uncles were hanging out. As soon as Theory got outside, he released his rage. He threw the trashcan and kicked whatever was in his path. "Ahhhhh!" he screamed.

"What's wrong?" their uncles chorused.

Before Valor could answer, Theory erupted again. "I can't stand him. He has no right to be here. He has no right to ask me for forgiveness. He violated me. Fathers protect their children. They don't abuse them. Nah, that ain't right. How he gonna ask me some ' *Why won't I let him love me*'? Because when I needed his love, he withheld it. That's why!" Theory shouted, showcasing the cords and veins from this throat to his muscled arms. He was livid.

Walker, the eldest of the Campbell brothers, hurried over. "Let it out, Theory; let it all out. Let the anger go. You kept it in a long time. Now let it all go," Walker spoke calmly and embraced him.

"I don't owe him nothing, Walker. It's been twenty-one years. My mama dead. I got a sister I've never met, and this dude really wants to act like he's father of the year," Theory fumed as his tears wetted his uncle's shirt. "Why didn't he just stay gone?"

"I know. I know, son."

"He gonna hurt my little sister, too. That's all he knows how to do. You know what dealers do to little girls?" The same sick thing Greg was doing to Virtuous, but that was coming to an end as well. He had enough of sick men.

"He won't, Theory. We won't let him. Be cool, okay? Today, we celebrate. You have your son and a beautiful girl that loves you. Ma made it through her stroke, and you found out you have a sister. We need to be thankful for all those blessings. This party is for Virtuous and Valor; let's be thankful."

Valor just looked on, helpless. He was shaking just as badly as Theory. Then large hands pulled him into an embrace. "He's going to be okay, son. That's years of pent-up emotions. He needs this cleansing," Gerald told Valor.

"I don't like seeing my brother like that. That's not just hurt, that's deeper. Uncle Stanley shouldn't have come here. I won't lose my brother because Stanley is looking for atonement."

"Valor, they're both hurt. I think now they can start the healing. Theory's going to need us, all of us. We'll help him stay on the right path. He's mourning his mother and his father. I can't imagine his pain, but we must love him through this."

Valor nodded.

A & Ω

Virtuous finally finished playing with the kids, and she looked around for Valor since he never came back for Tory. She was about to ask where he was when she heard a loud commotion. Something told her it was either Theory or Valor, and knowing that both of their fathers were present, she was prepared for a semi-blowup.

"Rika, come get Tory. I think something is going on up front."

Rika did as she was asked, and Virtuous took off toward the front of the house. Once she arrived, she was noticed that trash was everywhere, and everyone was in a different state of shock.

Virtuous looked around, searching for Theory and Valor and found Theory first. It was clear that he was upset. His uncles Luther, Clyde, Walker, and Baylor surrounded him. That caused Virtuous' belly to flop. Normally, she would just wait in the background, but something told her that he needed her, and he needed her now.

Marching forward, Virtuous squeezed through the circle to get to Theory, to her heart. "Theory, talk to me."

Theory looked up at her, but it was as if he did not see her. So, she cupped his face and pulled him down so that they were eye-to-eye, "Talk to me baby, please," she encouraged.

Instantly, his arms wrapped around her waist, and he buried his face into her neck. "I don't want to talk. I just want to hold you."

"Okay, whatever you need."

"I need you," Theory confessed.

CHAPTER 6

Staci split her time between Selma and Nocturnal, and it had taken a toll on her mentally. But after all, she had done, it was the least she could do. Sure, she was tired, but as a mother, there was nothing she would not do for her child. What renewed her energy was reading a passage in the Bible in 2 Corinthians (12:9-10). Staci had been meditating on that verse ever since Nocturnal was brought into the hospital.

Two wonderful things happened in the past three days: she finally met her father Zeno, and Selma's condition was improving.

Zeno and Staci ultimately had a real conversation, and he wanted to be in her life. And she needed him in it. Selma finally had a good prognosis. That was all God.

Staci's mother took Sadie back to Anderson, and Chauncory was doing well with his dad. Not that she spoke to Theory directly, but he did talk to Jenna and Sharifa. Theory let Chauncory call her in the mornings to say good morning and at night to recap his day and say goodnight. She could tell that Chauncory wholeheartedly loved Theory. Who could blame him? Theory really was a good man, and from what she could see in her son, a great father. All Chauncory talked about on the phone were all the fun things he and his dad did and how he loved his new family.

It brought Staci joy and pain. Her son could have had all of that since birth. She was learning to let go of the guilt and accept her past mistakes but not allow them to hold hostage her present. There was a song on the radio by Tenth Avenue North called "Healing Begins", which made her cry and praise God all at once. It was time for healing and forgiving.

Presently, she was in Nocturnal's hospital room. He was still in the ICU, but hopefully, he would be moved to a private room in another week. He had been in a medically induced coma that they were slowly bringing him out of. His was healing, but there had been multiple traumas to his body. They had to cut his beloved dreads before performing surgery on his brain to reduce the swelling. He no longer looked like the Nocturnal she once knew. Gone was the powerful aura that made him appear virtually immortal; now, he just looked like a lump of unused clay. The wreck that had taken Congo's life had also taken a part of Nocturnal's life.

Releasing a sigh, she started her daily routine. It was calming for her to keep busy and care for the father of her youngest children. First, she gave him a sponge bath. After that, she massaged his body with lotion, and finally, moisturized his lips with organic shea butter. Upon completing that task, she lifted his left hand, as the right had been burned in the wreck and was bandaged, and placed both her hands around his and prayed. Staci prayed for the healing of his body, mind, soul, as well for inner strength.

Life was going to change when Nocturnal awakened and he discovered that his best friend since his youth was dead. Congo was going to be buried in two days, and Nocturnal would most likely still be in his coma. Once he found out, it would break the remaining pieces of his heart. That worried Staci because not only had he lost his son, but now, his best friend. With all that loss and his refusal to accept Christ in his life, she had no idea how he would survive mentally or emotionally.

To add insult to injury, Penelope and Priscilla were distant, but Staci suspected that after the way they verbally attacked her. She held no ill will. There was no room for that now. Hate and self-loathing had no place in her heart or life. There was too much to be thankful for than to worry about the people and situations she could not change.

At the end of the day, Staci was thankful that they stayed with Selma while she was with Nocturnal, and when she was with Selma, they sat with Nocturnal. Staci continued to pray that soon, the anger, pain, and fear that were felt would ease, and they would better for it.

A & Ω

Nora wiped her tear-stained face. She had been crying for days. Recently, she learned that she was pregnant, and she knew that at six weeks Nocturnal was not the father but his best friend Congo. Congo did not know about her creeping with Nocturnal behind his back. It was only that one time, but she had been lusting after Nocturnal for a while. After he flipped on her for coming after Staci, she knew that he was not the man for her. So, she had tried to focus on getting into Congo's good graces. But now, he was dead, and she sadly found comfort in Congo not knowing how horrible she really was. Theory was right when he called her foul.

It still did not seem real. Congo was gone, and she had no way to financially support herself and his child. Her gravy train was no longer alive, and she could not find a new sponsor while with a child.

Nora was tempted to go and get the abortion pill. At six weeks, she still had time; in fact, from her research, she had up to ten weeks to terminate the pregnancy. It seemed the reasonable action to take as she could not see the financial benefit of having a child with no father. Being on government assistance was not even an option. Her mother was on assistance when she was a child and she never forgot that feeling. The way people looked at them and the judgment she felt, was something she never wanted again.

Nora's mind drifted back to the conversation she had months ago. She had been critical and cruel about Staci having three children and being unmarried. Now she was in an even worse situation.

Before Nora could get lost in thoughts of depression and sorrow, there was a knock at her door. Letting out a sigh, she cleaned her face and went to answer the door. She looked out the peephole and saw Maisha. The two had not spoken in a while, but that was more Nora's doing than Maisha's. Smoothing out her clothing, she unlocked and opened the door.

"Hey, Mai."

"Hey, Nora, may I come in?"

Nora stood aside and welcomed her into the house. Maisha entered and quickly sat down on the couch.

"So?" Nora replied to fill in the awkward silence.

"Well, first off, Nora, I apologize for not coming to check on you earlier. We drifted and that was as much my fault as yours. I'm not angry with you or anything like that. It's just that you chose Congo. You know how you get when you set your sights a guy. You forget your friends. In this situation, my cousin Theory has or had a conflict with Congo and Nocturnal. I know you wanted to be down for him, but I'll forever be loyal to my family. However, our friendship should have been able to withstand that. If after this, you choose to no longer engage with me, I'll respect your decision."

Nora had to smile. Maisha was different. She was changing or maybe, this was always who she was and she simply changed to fit in with Nora. "I miss us."

Maisha nodded. "I came to check on you. I was told that you're pregnant and that the baby belongs to Congo. With his funeral just two days away, I thought you could use some emotional support."

Before Maisha finished talking, Nora was in tears. "I don't know what to do. A baby doesn't fit into my plan. I'm seriously considering having an abortion."

Maisha's eyes widened at her revelation. "Please don't. I know I have no right to speak on this, but Congo was his mother's only child. From what I hear, she isn't taking his death well at all. Maybe this pregnancy is a blessing in disguise because Willamina can still have a piece of her son in her grandchild."

"I don't want a baby."

"Just tell Willamina that you're pregnant. I'm sure she'll want the baby and will support you until you give birth. Abortion is not the only option; just let her adopt the baby. That way, you still have your life and that child has its life. There's no need to cause another death," Maisha spoke boldly.

Nora sniffled but she nodded at her friend's reasoning. Most people would say she was selfish and a little devious. And she would have to agree. No one would ever believe she would do something merciful for anyone else. Plus, later in life, she wanted to have children—with the right wealthy man.

"Are you okay?" Maisha asked.

"Yes, and I think you're right. Can you ride with me to see Congo's mother? I would like to pay my respects and share with her that she has a grandchild on the way."

Maisha smiled. "Really?"

"Really."

A & Ω

Ezekiel was shaken after Penelope told him that Nocturnal had been in a severe car accident that could possibly paralyze him for life. His heart mourned Congo who was being buried tomorrow. Congo was a good dude, and he hated that he died so young. Ezekiel wanted to be there for the family and show support, but these bars had him caged and helpless for a few more months.

Letting out a frustrated sigh, Ezekiel turned his attention back to Penelope. She was on his piss list after what she did to her own brother.

"Nel, why didn't you tell Noc that Chauncory wasn't his son? You knew from the jump, yet you kept that from him for five years. I can't believe you," Ezekiel blasted her.

Ezekiel was not the one on that deceitful and disloyal mindset. Her actions had him wondering if she was keeping secrets like that from him.

Finally, he stared up at her and at least she had the good sense to look guilty and ashamed.

"I just, I mean, it's not my fault. They were in love, and Chauncory fit, so how could I tell my brother, his firstborn, his only son, that his son wasn't his? It wasn't my place to shatter his world."

He shook his head in disagreement. "It really was, though. I better never find out you're holding secrets from me. I would lose my mind," he snapped.

"What secrets could I possibly be keeping from you?" she questioned.

"I don't know. Apparently, the secret of your brother's son not being his son."

Penelope dropped her head. Shaking his own, he did his best to calm down. He needed to share with her the information he found out. "We'll table that for now because I have something to tell you." At that, her head popped up and when she noticed how serious he looked, her face mirrored his.

"What?"

Ezekiel took a deep breath and then exhaled before revealing that his twins were alive. "At first, I thought it was a lie. Then, I was like, why would this white lady be contacting me unless there was some truth to this? I have fraternal twins. They're eighteen now, a girl and a boy. I looked them up, too. My daughter is an art prodigy; she got that from Valerie. Her mother could paint like Goethe Pemba. Then, my son, he's like this phenom athlete. He plays every sport. He got that from me. Both are highly intelligent and excel in school. My lawyer got a file for me. I sent them the form, so they can come see me and hopefully meet Evie and Evan."

Ezekiel knew it would be a shock to Penelope, but he was unprepared for her tears. Something just felt off about her reaction.

"Babe, you good?"

"I thought you said that Valerie had an abortion."

"That's what she told me she was going to do after she left me. Her father, once he found out she was pregnant by a black man, a street dude at that, demanded she kill my seeds. He had her on a total blackout. I couldn't get any information on her. When she died, and they found her body in Anderson, that just blew my mind. I still don't understand what happened. I can't get a straight story for nothing.

"She overdosed," Penelope deadpanned.

"Yeah, but why? Valerie was a health nut. She would've never voluntarily put poison in her body."

"Well, she did!"

Ezekiel shut his mouth and just glared at Penelope. "Nel, don't be jealous of a dead woman. I can't stand when you act like that. That's my children's mother. Chill out. You're my wife, so don't start acting petty. I'm not in the mood."

"I ain't in the mood either!"

Ezekiel narrowed his eyes at her outburst, and she had the good sense to simmer down.

"I'm sorry. I just don't understand why you keep bringing her up. She's been dead for years, and y'all been over for longer. You're acting like this is fresh or whatever."

That pissed him off. It *was* fresh. The pain did not ease. "It *is* fresh! I just found out the children I thought were dead are alive. A piece of the woman I deeply cared about is still out there. I'm sharing that with my wife because my twins are your children, too, and the brother and sister of our children."

"What if they don't want a relationship with us? Then what?"

"Then I have to respect that, but I'm going to reach out and do my best to convince them."

Penelope shook her head. "You know, after that woman left you, you went dark, and I had to fight to bring you back. I just don't want to lose you like that again, Ezekiel. I love you so much."

Ezekiel nodded. Penelope had loved him for a long time. However, he was ten years her senior and only saw her as an immature young woman. Then, after Valerie left him, Penelope was there—every, single day. She stood by him even when he didn't want her. After a while, he saw her as more than just the sister of one of his soldiers. He fell for her, but what he felt for her wasn't what he felt for Valerie. He loved that woman, still did, but he would never tell Penelope that. Her mental could not handle that level of honesty.

"I know, baby. I lost my mind, but you were there. I'm not going to lose it again. My children, all four of them, are important to me, and I need you to respect that. If the twins choose not to meet me then I'll let it be. What I won't do is be less than to you or our children," he assuaged her.

CHAPTER 7

Virtuous finished cleaning her art supplies and headed out of the art room. As she was getting into her crossover, her cell phone started to ring. It was a number unknown to her, but she answered it just in case it involved Ezekiel.

"Hello. May I speak with Virtuous All?"

"Yes, this is Virtuous. Who's speaking?"

"This is Nadel Wentworth. I'm contacting you on behalf of my client, Ezekiel All."

"Yes, is it possible for us to set up a time to meet? I would like my brother to hear what you have to say as well. He and I attend different schools and have different schedules; however, we would both like to speak to you and learn more about Mr. All."

"Of course. I thought it would be a good idea to perform a DNA test on you both before proceeding. I just need to ensure you're both his children."

"I agree, and I'm sure Valor will as well."

"Great. How about you call me back tomorrow, and we can go from there?"

"Sure. Thank you."

"Thank you!" Nadel replied and hung up.

After that, Virtuous quickly texted Valor and then headed to meet up with Theory. It seemed that he and Chauncory blended easily. It was as if they were never separated, and that elated Virtuous. Theory had also let go of the anger and hurt he felt toward Grammy, Staci, and her family. Right now, he was not budging on his feelings, or feelings lack thereof, for Stanley. Virtuous was not going to push it.

Less than half an hour later, Virtuous was pulling up at Grammy's house, just as Theory was leaving out. His son was now attending the Christian school where Cheryl, Walker's wife, was the principal and made the transition for Chauncory seamless.

"Proverbs, baby, I didn't think I'd see you today," Theory greeted her, followed by his trademark grin, which made her smile as well.

When Theory truly smiled, his entire demeanor change. He was a gorgeous man.

"I missed you and I needed to check on my boys. Where's Chauncory?"

"Trek came and got him to take him to spend the night with his sister and Sharifa. I'm going to pick him up Saturday night."

Virtuous smiled and fell into Theory's opened arms. "You feel so good," Theory whispered in her ear. She felt the same way about him, which was why she lingered in his embrace longer than necessary.

"You do, too. You smell so good. Do you do any work at work?" Virtuous teased as she inhaled his scent.

"You better know it. Come on and talk to me," Theory requested as he offered his hand for her to hold.

Virtuous was glad to see that Theory was looking better, calmer. The past week had been rough on him from the Staci situation to his father's arrival. However, with the grace of God, he was still standing, and she was thankful, yet again, that Grammy raised him to be a man of God and not a man of men.

"Theory, I came because I want to apologize to you. It was my idea for your fa—, I mean, for Stanley to come to church. My plan was to warn you ahead of time so that you wouldn't be surprised. Then everything with Chauncory and the car accident happened, and I was unable to get a hold of you. I feel like that breakdown between you two was my fault."

Theory shook his head in disagreement. "Stop. That wasn't your fault. You were only trying to help, and besides, Grammy told me all about it. She said you straight up threatened them. I talked to Uncle Gerald, and he was like, '*Your girlfriend is sweet and all, but that little lady has some fire and sass in her when it comes to you and Valor*'. I was like, yep."

Virtuous giggled. "I love you guys."

"I know, and we love you, too. I appreciate you having my back, but that Stanley situation won't be resolved overnight. I've said what I needed to say for now. I just want to chill with my sister and possibly reach out to Angela's side of the family in North Carolina. I never knew they even existed."

It surprised her at how light his voice became when he spoke about his mother's relatives. There was hope glistening in his eyes, and she prayed it all worked out. "Really? That would be great. I love North

Carolina. That's where I want to attend college. Well, I did until Greg decided that if I moved, he was coming, too."

Theory tensed and tightened his grip on her hand. Virtuous let out a low hiss from the discomfort. Had she been thinking, she would have never brought up Greg, Theory had enough to deal with, without her inviting her demons to the table. "Theory?"

"Sorry but I really can't stand that man. I've never met him, but I wholeheartedly dislike him for what he's done to you."

"I know. I should've never brought that up," Virtuous apologized, instantly feeling guilty and wishing she could take back the part about Greg. Life had been somewhat of a fairy-tale while he was away on his hunting trip.

Theory let out a harsh breath as he and Virtuous walked around to the back of the house. "Let's take Logic for his walk. We need to chat."

Virtuous did not respond verbally, but she nodded her agreement. Quietly, she watched Theory interact with the puppy and put on his walking leash, and then he reached for her hand again as the two started plodding toward the road.

"What's on your mind?" Virtuous asked after five minutes of unbearable silence, at least on her part. It was easier for her when she was helping Theory deal with his issues. Then, she could forget all about her own, but right now, she was feeling the pressure.

"Funny because I was going to ask what's on yours? Honestly, Val and I have noticed that something is up with you. You've been like that since Grammy went into the hospital, and before you fix your mouth to deny it, we don't keep secrets," he quickly reminded her.

Virtuous really did not want to tell him because it would only create a more hostile situation, and she was unprepared for that. All she wanted was to be done with it all. Now, with Addison reaching out to Ezekiel, she had no idea how this mess was going to play out.

"Virtuous, why are you crying?" Theory asked, concerned.

She had not noticed tears were falling until Theory asked her. Instead of answering, she just rested her hand in his upper arm.

"Baby, what's wrong?" He gently caressed her.

Sighing, Virtuous replied, "I don't want to upset you."

"What have I told you about giving me that line? Just tell me because when you keep stuff from me, even if you think it's good to keep something from me, it's bad and upsetting. I don't like it."

"Can we go back to the house?"

He nodded and when they arrived at the house, he let Logic loose while they sat on the back steps. "Tell me."

Virtuous dropped her head. "Proverbs, don't do that."

She lifted her head and said a quick prayer mentally before answering him. "A couple of weeks ago, I woke up to Greg in my bedroom. He questioned me about the bracelet you bought and about my art project. Finally, I was just like, you know, I want to stay with Mamaw until I graduate and go off to college."

"That's when he told you he was going to move to whatever you went to school?" Theory concluded, ticked off.

"No, he'd done that a long time ago. What he said was that I had to come back home in December. He added that if I didn't, the games he used to play with me, he would start playing with Maddison and Tory."

Theory did a triple take before speaking. "Say what? I think I misheard you." Virtuous knew he heard her just fine because his eyes were dilating, and his nostrils were flaring. He had his fist so tight she thought his skin would rip open.

"He threatened to abuse the girls. Don't be mad," Virtuous pleaded.

"*Don't be mad?*" An incredulous glare tattooed his face. "Virtuous, those are innocent, helpless babies. I love them, girls. Tory is like my own daughter, and Cutie is like a sister. My goodness, Cutie isn't that much older than Cordy. Nah, Proverbs, we gotta do something. You and the girls aren't going back to him," Theory snapped.

"I agree. I have a month to make my moves, but I got a call the other day and today."

Theory frowned but must have noticed the weary look on Virtuous' face because his frown eased. "What kind of calls?"

"Well, the day you left to get Chauncory, a man called me, claiming he was my and Valor's father. He even told me that Addison came to see him because he thought our birth mother had aborted us. Then today, before I came to see you, his lawyer called and wanted to set up a time to meet, take a DNA test, and then go from there. I texted Valor and he said he wanted to do it soon. Maybe, if Greg is aware that I have a family then he'll back off."

The anger Theory tried to tame was back, and it was pulsating. Virtuous could see the vein in his neck thumping. It pained her to put him through this after what he had to deal with just yesterday. "I'm sorry. I thought if I told you about Greg while Grammy was in the hospital, you would freak out. I just didn't want to burden you."

Theory jerked from her hold and glared at her. "Stop doing that, Virtuous. We don't keep secrets from each other. You love reminding me of that, but you're quick to forget it! I'm your man. I don't need you to coddle and protect me like a baby. My mental isn't weak, okay. Yeah, Grammy having that stroke scared me, but baby, you're being violated by Greg. He put his hands on you, and you not telling me hurts a lot more. Do you think I can't protect you?"

"No." Virtuous shook her head to make sure he understood that.

"Are you sure? I can't tell. It seems to me that you're protecting Greg. This fool threatened to sexually abuse your daughter and your sister, and you do nothing. That's the same thing Addison did to you. That blows my mind." Theory turned his back and placed his hands on his head. It was evident that he was exasperated by the situation—and with her.

"I'm not like Addison and never say that again! I did do something Theory!" she fumed. "I called Serena, but she's on sabbatical, so I can't speak to her. I did tell Tamari, and that was huge for me."

"What can either of them do about your current situation? How is that helpful? That's pissing me off, Virtuous. Your protection of him is provoking me. If you want the abuse to end, then you *need* to do something. You're eighteen now, so there aren't any excuses."

Virtuous did her best not to cry, but she knew he was pissed because he rarely called her Virtuous. His aggravation with her made her nervous, and his tone and way he spoke to her were harsh. Feeling thoroughly chastised, all she could say was, "I'm sorry."

"No! No more apologies." Theory clapped his hands to express his displeasure. "They don't mean anything unless there's a behavioral change with it. So, you better tell that cop that Grammy knows; you better tell the school nurse, the school social worker, the sheriff, or somebody because I'm done with the anxiety. Every time you leave me, I wonder if he's forcing himself on you. Is he beating you? Jason can't watch you 24/7, and if you move back into that house, you know what he'll do. Something has to change, or we ain't goin' make it," Theory lectured, frustrated.

"What?" Virtuous went completely numb. Never in their relationship had Theory ever taken such a chiding tone with her. The threat of him leaving her, letting her go, was terrifying. No one had ever been in her corner like him.

"You heard me, Virtuous. Stop being scared and hiding behind the fact that he's a cop and speak up. Greg is a man, just like any other; he's not indestructible. The only power he has is the power you give him. You can destroy him—so do it! Right now, your silence is protecting Greg, and I'm not supporting that."

Every word Theory spoke felt like a physical slash on her body. "You'd break up with me? Like, you'd just leave me because I'm not moving at your pace?" she spluttered. Her heart nearly broke at what he was suggesting.

"I love you, Proverbs. One day, I hope to marry you, adopt Tory, and all of us be a big, happy family. I really want that. However, I can't be your man and not step up like a man and handle that punk. You won't let me come for him, and you won't advocate for yourself, so what am I to do?"

Blindsided by his reaction, Virtuous had to admit that Theory's point was valid. The way he stared at her let her know he was serious. She was going to lose the only man she ever loved. A man that saw beauty in her ugliness and survival in her scars. It was torturing her soul.

Sighing, she dropped her eyes, defeated. Finally, she responded, "You're right, Theory. There's a lot going on in your life with Stanley. You're dealing with losing your mother, finding out about your sister, and discovering that you have a son. You don't need my drama. So, we'll just take a break. You do your life, and I'll do mine." God knows she was lying. No parts of her wanted to be without Theory, but he did not sign up for her life problems. As much as it was breaking her entire being, at least letting him go would save his life.

Nodding her head as if that sealed her fate, she got up and started to walk away from a flummoxed Theory.

"Virtuous Atarah All, you better be exercising and not leaving. Don't play with me like that. I'm pissed off and I'm emotional. However, if you walk away from me, don't you ever walk back to me. If you abandon me like my parents did then you'll be dead to me."

His words felt like a whip had slashed her physically. The emotion in his voice pierced her heart. Virtuous halted mid-step, her shoulders shaking as she became overwhelmed by his ultimatum. Slowly, she turned around to face him. A gut-wrenching scream fought to escape, but she pushed it down. Not one part of her ever wanted to harm Theory. The look of desperation on his face and the terror in his eyes was going to kill her.

Theory was beyond upset, but she also saw his raw pain and fear. It shattered her heart.

"What can I do? I love you, Theory; you know that. You're *my heart*. I've done all that I can to protect *my heart*. I'm not protecting Greg or, at least, that's not my intention," Virtuous blurted as she tasted her salty tears. "I'm tired, Theory, and I'm afraid. I don't want my problems to become your problems. Yes, I want you safe, and no, it's not because I don't think you can't protect yourself or me. It's because Greg doesn't play fair. Because if I lose my heart, how do I live?" Doing her best not to drop her head, she added, "You have Chauncory and Cordy now; they need you. If I make a wrong step that impacts you then you could lose all of that. I'm not worth that, Theory. I can't let you lose anymore. God knows I would never abandon you, but I don't know what to do," Virtuous confessed, now desperate.

"So, you're the sacrifice?" His face flushed with grief as he took one step closer to her.

"I am. I can't live without my heart, but a heart can live in someone else. Right?"

Theory shook his head. "Nope, it's not going down like that, Proverbs. It's you, or it's no one. Do you remember the story of Abraham and Isaac? Didn't God provide another sacrifice? He'll do that now, too. Whatever happened to prayer and believing in God. It's faith over fear, Proverbs."

"God doesn't hear me anymore, Theory. I've been too indecisive!" she screamed, as speaking had become draining. Everything that she had buried, the lies, the pain, the abuse, was finally coming out. Every fear, the wavering faith she had in God, was showing. She just wanted it all to go away.

"He doesn't hear me. Maybe He never did. My faith is failing, okay? It's hard to pray to Him when every time I close my eyes, all I see is the man who has abused me. It's difficult. I do my best to believe, but…"

"Aw, baby, please don't start doubting God. Not now. We've come too far, and He has done too much for you to doubt Him. I'm not letting you give up on God, and I know you wouldn't let me.

"I'm sorry I lost my temper, but the idea of Greg hurting Tory and Cutie like he's done you just sent me over the edge. I'm not losing you, and Greg can't have you." Theory cupped her face and rubbed their noses together. Virtuous' hands rested on his wrist, and she closed her eyes and slowly inhaled the scent of him.

"He can't hurt them now. He's in the hospital, healing from two gunshot wounds. There was an accident while they were hunting."

"Well, that gives us some time to think of something. Just please don't give up. Don't walk away from God or me," he pleaded, pulling her into a deep embrace. "Don't leave me."

"I'll keep my word, but if this is too much, you can let me go. I'll face it all alone to keep you safe."

"Nah, we forever and always, Proverbs. We're in this together. I'll always be your heart."

CHAPTER 8

The hip hop beats of Andy Mineo played in the background as Theory and his friends hung out. The guys had come over to chill and just catch up after a whirlwind week. It was what Theory needed, and he knew that Virtuous was kicking it with Tamari. She needed a break, too.

Everything was just too tense.

Theory was thankful his friends were over, now, because the explosive blowup between him and Proverbs bothered him immensely. So much so that he reached out to Jason who assured him he would stay close to the girls. Also, Jason shared that Greg would not be allowed to fly home until next week. They still had some time, but not much, to make some plans.

"Y'all, Yulonda tried it today. I told her to stop all that playing with me or I was going to Joshua, Chapter 6 her," Archie fussed as he dealt out the cards.

Shalamar glanced up at Archie with a bewildered gaze. "What?"

"Man, you know in Joshua, Chapter 6, *The Destruction of Jericho*, for one week, they marched around the city and destroyed it. I told Lon I was going to do that if she kept entertaining them dudes."

"Whoa, she was stepping out on you? I didn't get CHOT vibes from her," Theory clarified, spitting out the shell of the sunflower seed. He had never gotten that vibe from her. However, if she were that type then she could not be around Virtuous or his cousins.

"Nah, my baby ain't a CHOT. She's been tutoring athletes from the football team. I told her she needed to do that at the school library and not at her apartment. We not finna do that. One of them fools try to get frisky with my lady, and I'm going to have to catch a charge. Y'all know I'm saved now; I can't be in *Jail Birds*," Archie explained, screwing up his face.

Valor fell over laughing. "Really, Archie? This dude for real in love."

"My man, you a whole nutcase over there. I'm getting my BSW, so you know I know," Shalamar teased.

Theory shook his head. "Only you would have thought of something like that. I bet homeboy thought you were outta yo mind."

"I marched around that entire apartment, and homie ducked out of there so fast he left his textbooks. I thought ol' boy was *The Flash*."

They all laughed, and Theory fell on the floor laughing. It felt so good to laugh after the intense argument he had with Proverbs.

Getting himself back together, he dusted off his clothing and sat back down. "You're a whole fool for that, Archie. What Yulonda say after all that?"

"Then I sat down and turned on the television. I patted the couch for Lon to sit beside me, and we watched *Black-ish* on demand. She watched that show with me and ordered some food. I reminded Yulonda that I'm for real about us. Yeah, I like to laugh but don't mistake laughter for weakness, and don't let the light skin fool you. Everybody be sleeping on the light-skinned brothers like we don't get down," he added before sipping his sweet iced tea.

"That poor girl. Does she have any thick, dark-skinned cousins or best friends? I'm asking for myself," Shalamar stated, making everyone laugh again.

They goofed off a little more before starting the next round of spades.

A & Ω

The serenade of beeping machinery and Nocturnal's constant breathing played in the background as Staci tucked her feet under her. She had attended Congo's funeral in Anderson then saw Chauncory before driving back down to Atlanta to be with Nocturnal and Selma. Her sister Jenna was sitting with Selma while Staci went to check on Nocturnal. It was a thankless and tiresome job, but Staci felt like she owed this to Nocturnal. They had both hurt each other terribly. However, once the anger settled, Staci knew hers was more with herself and not with Nocturnal. If she were honest, she still had feelings for him. Maybe not love, as in being in love, but she did not want this to ever happen to him.

Staci was sitting in the chair, knitting and humming to herself when the bed started to stir. This had happened before as Nocturnal would move his body but not open his eyes. It seemed to her that he was trying to either get up or communicate. The doctor was hopeful that he would wake soon. When nothing else happened, Staci returned to knitting. She was making little booties for Selma and a scarf for Sadie. It was something she learned how to do after joining her new church.

"Ma?"

Staci lifted her head at the sound of Nocturnal's raspy voice. It sounded dry and painful, like how sandpaper would sound if it had a voice. Setting her knitting aside, she rose from the chair and cautiously ambled over to him. Staci knew in her heart that she was most likely the last person he wanted to see, but she was, or at least she hoped, prepared for his temper.

"Noc, Priscilla isn't here, but I can call her."

His features wrinkled as he recognized her voice, but his eyes were still fighting to open. She prayed that when they did, he would not go into shock. His body had been through enough trauma, and she did not want to add to the mental damage on top of the physical damage he had suffered.

Hesitantly, she touched her unmanicured hand to his chest, her mind instantly flashing back to better times when love reigned and not uncertainty. However, as quickly as it came, it left. Her intention was to sooth Nocturnal, but instead, it only increased his distress, and she abruptly lifted her hand. Staci mentally chastised herself. She should have known that Nocturnal did not want her touch. Why should he? "I'm sorry Noc, for everything," she whispered closing her eyes.

When her eyes opened, they clashed with his dark orbs. All she saw was bitterness and loathing. He hated her. There was no doubt about it. It was a feeling she knew well because, at one time, she hated him, too. Now, she could not gather those horrible emotions for anything. What she felt for him now was probably worse than hate; she felt pity and sorrow.

As Staci began to step away, his uninjured hand grabbed her, alarming her by its strength. Then again, he was fueled by agony and animosity. "Percival," she stated calmly. Her eyes traveled down the white blanket, and his eyes followed. There was an empty space on one side of the bed. His right leg had been amputated at the knee, and he would need a prosthetic.

It was then she felt the life drain out of him. His grip on her slackened, and she knew he realized that he wasn't the same anymore.

"Leg?"

Staci winced. *Why couldn't Priscilla or Penelope be here to explain this?* she mentally questioned.

"You lost half of it in the wreck. They were not able to reattach it, but with physical therapy and the use of a prosthetic, you'll be like your old self."

He glared daggers at her, but she was his only lifeline, and she knew he had questions. "Congo?"

At the sound of his name, tears ran, unchecked, down her face. "He, he didn't make it. His funeral was today." Before she could properly explain, Nocturnal let out a painful roar that could have awakened the dead. He started thrashing in his bed, probably causing himself more harm, but he did not seem to care. It was breaking her heart. Never had she seen Nocturnal like this. He was strong and courageous; he was tough and relentless. He always seemed more than human, and now, he was weak and broken. Just a man, just an ordinary man.

Staci quickly paged the nurse and called for assistance. Then she grabbed her cell phone and sent a text to Priscilla and Penelope. They were supposed to be here later as they were in Anderson with Willamina. They were needed now.

Staci eased into the background, guilt gnawing at her. This time, instead of becoming overwhelmed, she just prayed.

CHAPTER 9

Nocturnal felt as if someone steamrolled over him with an entire fleet of loaded tractor-trailers. For days, he had been in a dreamless abyss of pain and despair. His throat was dry and rough; breathing hurt, and moving was a challenge. Something just felt alien about his body.

Cautiously, his eyes flickered open and even that was painful, but he wanted to see, knowing that he was not in his room alone. He had thought he awakened before and saw Staci, but that must be his mind playing tricks on him. No way was she that stupid to be near him, but where was he?

"Noc, baby, it's Mama."

Finally! He had been calling her forever. "Ma, where am I?" his hoarse voice questioned. It was so foreign to him that he was a bit startled by the gravelly sound of it. Everything about him felt weird—and wrong.

"Hold on, let me get you some water," she prompted and poured him a cup from the plastic pitcher sitting on his tray. After she cleaned him up, she told attempted to explain everything. "You're in the hospital. You were speeding, and the police were trying to stop you, but you collided into an eighteen-wheeler and…" Priscilla trailed off. She couldn't speak any more from the sadness that grew thicker with each word.

"What happened? Where's Congo?" Nocturnal asked, his voice on fire as he asked questions. He knew that Congo would be in the room. Maybe he was out getting something to eat or flirting with a nurse.

"Baby, after you all had that wreck, there was too much damage, and everyone's injuries were severe. Congo didn't survive the wreck."

Nocturnal leaned his head to the left, thinking that he had heard his Mama wrong. "Dead?"

"Yes. Willamina buried him yesterday."

Nocturnal started to violently shake his head and thrash his body again. "Stop that, baby. They'll dope you up again, and we'll have to do this all over again. Listen to me, baby; he's gone, but it wasn't your fault. You were upset over Staci lying to you about Chauncory's paternity. I know it hurts, baby, but please be calm."

"Staci was here."

"Yes, she would sit and take care of you. She told me that she explained about Congo dying and about your leg."

"My leg?"

Nocturnal looked down at his leg, or what was left of it, and lost it again.

A & Ω

Penelope had been stressed. Between her brother, losing Congo, and Ezekiel's dead children coming back to life, she was barely making it. The only person she could confide in was Staci, but they were currently not on the best terms. However, now that some time had passed, Penelope viewed things differently. Besides, she did her dirt, too, and if Ezekiel ever found out, her life would cease to exist.

Picking up the phone, she quickly dialed Staci.

"Hello?" The voiced sounded frantic and surprised.

"Staci, it's Penelope. I'm sorry about how I've been treating you. It was just grief- and fear-talking."

"Apology accepted. I understand how the situation was and still is stressful."

"Good. Thank you. I need to speak to you."

"About?"

"About my situation. Can you come over? Are you still in Anderson or are you in Atlanta?"

"I'm in Anderson, visiting with Chauncory before he goes back to Theory."

"Well, we can meet afterward. I don't want to interrupt your time with Chauncey."

"I'll just come see you. Chauncory is over here playing with Sadie and some of his friends, so I can slip away for about an hour."

"Okay, well, my kids aren't here, so just come on over."

Less than twenty minutes later, there was a knock at Penelope's door, and she knew that it was Staci. She quickly ran to answer it.

"Come in."

Staci entered and settled down on the sofa. Penelope offered her a drink and something to eat, but Staci declined both. It was then Penelope noticed how different Staci looked. It was like she aged a lifetime. She had lost weight, but it looked unhealthy. Her hair was in a messy bun with several inches of new growth. Overall, her body just looked tired. Selma's health and Nocturnal's situation was definitely taking a toll on her.

"What do you need, Penelope?"

"I think I should be asking you that. Are you taking care of yourself?"

"Doing my best, but I have three children living in three different places. My ex hates me, and I sort of blame myself for his best friend's death. One minute, I feel strong, I read a verse, and I'm like, Lord, you got this. Then, the next moment, I feel like I can't move. All that progress was lost. I have a great church family back in Atlanta. I'll get better. However, that's not why I'm here. Tell me what you need to say."

Penelope felt guiltier now. Taking a deep breath, she began to talk. "I messed up, Staci. I let my jealousy get the best of me."

Staci grimaced, perplexed.

"Valerie never had an abortion. Some woman contacted Ezekiel and told him that his children are alive, and now, he's reaching out to them."

"So, why is that bad? I don't understand."

"Let me just start from the beginning. I've always been in love with Ezekiel, but he was a decade older than me and did not see me in that way. He was in love with Valerie, the twins' mother. I tried to sabotage their relationship, but that girl wasn't leaving. When I found out she was pregnant, I knew I had to get rid of her. I knew that her daddy was on the racist side, or at least, he did not approve of his daughter being with a black man. I contacted him and dropped that information. He was livid and told her to abort the pregnancy. She, in turn, told Ezekiel that her father demanded she terminate the pregnancy, and he lost it. Then Valerie disappeared. I thought she had an abortion and went on with her life. Ezekiel went dark, but I was there for him. We fell in love. Well, that heffa popped back up, but she was on something. Her mind was different. Even in her mental state, she wanted my man. I was not losing him." Penelope paused and swallowed hard as she relived the night that altered so many lives.

"What did you do?" Staci edged off the couch.

"I set it up. I used Vicious to end Valerie. He didn't rob her, I did. He was too far gone himself to recall anything. It was easy, really. We were dressed similarly, and the woman was already on something, so robbing her was like stealing candy from a baby. I left Vicious and put the money and ID on him and then called the police. Just in case it came back, I didn't want Ezekiel after me.

"Vicious was a juvenile, and I knew he wouldn't get any hard time. That should have scared her, but nope. She came back, even after I told her that Ezekiel had children with me. I told her that he loved me. I explained that she wasn't meant to be a street wife. She said she needed to tell him something then she would leave, but I didn't believe her. So, I let her think he was coming and, God forgive me, I…"

"You overdosed her," Staci finished. "Whoa…wait, you set up Theory? Like, you did that? I thought you made him rob her. You set him up, not just to get arrested but to get handled by Ezekiel? I really thought he committed a crime. He's innocent. What did Theory ever do to you? He lost six years of his life because of your deception! He missed the birth of our son, and you did all of this to keep Ezekiel? Penelope, you killed an innocent woman."

"Innocent? I don't know about that, but yeah, I assisted in her death," Penelope snapped. "It would have stayed forever buried except for the fact that his kids are still alive. And now, sleeping dogs are awake and sniffing. What can I do?"

"Tell the truth, to Ezekiel, Theory, and the police."

Penelope shook her head. "Girl, that's too much truth-telling. Try again."

"You saw what me keeping the truth from Nocturnal has done; why do the same? Just tell Ezekiel. I can tell Theory. I don't understand why you chose Theory, though."

Penelope's dark brown eyes turned black. She jumped up as if she was preparing to fight Staci, and Staci stood, prepared to defend herself. "No, Staci, no. Just let me handle this. I chose Theory because he wanted to be down. It was time for him to prove himself, but after he was released, he wanted nothing to do with street life."

Staci shook her head. "Ezekiel still could hurt him. Are you crazy? This won't end well if you don't tell the truth. This is God warning you, Penelope. Do the right thing before it all blows up in your face. That's my advice. I know you're scared, but you'll feel better once the truth is out. I can promise you that." After saying her piece, Staci grabbed her purse and made her exit.

A & Ω

Theory knocked on the door and waited for Virtuous to let him in. He missed her, so after picking up Chauncory from Sharifa's house, he headed over to see Virtuous.

"Coming," her dulcet voice serenaded.

A second later the door was opened, and Theory was presented with her beautiful smile that warmed him. Chauncory perked up the moment he saw her, too, and ran into her arms. He and little buddy were going to have a conversation about his blocking.

"Did you make cupcakes?" Chauncory asked, and she nodded. That caused him to leap up and down and then he took off as if he knew where he was going.

Theory shook his head before turning his attention back to Virtuous. "Hey, Proverbs."

"Hey," she cheesed, embracing him. "C'mon in and get settled. I was hoping we could watch *Beyond the Lights*. I love that movie. Jason will entertain the kids. I figured we could get a little alone time." She wiggled her eyebrows making a goofy face that had him chuckling.

Theory liked that idea. He entered the house and waited for her to shut the door and then kissed the top of her nose. "I'm sorry about our disagreement. I know I apologized already, but it bothers me that I hurt you. I never want to hurt you. I'm the one that's supposed to love you through whatever, and I dropped the ball. When you're ready to speak your truth then I'll be there to support you."

Virtuous fell into his arms and burrowed deeper into his embrace. "I want to be free of him, Theory. You're right about me protecting him. I've let my fear lead and not my faith. Fear has had me questioning God. So, I've been reading the Bible a lot. I've been in deep prayer, fasting, and meditating. I can't be fearful and faithful because those two things work in different directions. Fear, unless it's a good fear, leads to self-destruction, and before you entered my life, that was my path. I was living in fear and not in faith. Our argument was tough to hear, but it was necessary." She took a deep breath, exhaled, and looked into his eyes. It was almost as if she could see through his soul. They were that deeply bonded.

"*Faith* in Hebrews states 'Now faith is the substance of things hoped for, the evidence of things not seen'." I need to have faith that God knows my pain, my struggle, and my fears. I need to believe that all those times I thought He was ignoring me He was rebuilding me. All my life I've felt disconnected, separated in a way that others aren't. I never knew my bio-parent. My soul yearned, for years, for a brother I kept locked in my heart so that the ugliness I suffered wouldn't destroy my memories of him. Then I gave birth to Tory. My little Victory. I named her that because I wanted her to be victorious, even if I wasn't. Then God gave me you. I started to feel renewed. I felt like there's somebody who sees me, not my brokenness, not my damage, but just Virtuous. Maybe, I'm somebody worthy. I got addicted to having something that was all my own. Then I met Valor and the rest of your family, and I never want to lose that. Once Greg threatened me and the girls, all I saw was losing everything I gained. I didn't want to lose that love. I've been unloved for a long time, and the thought of losing any of you, well, it was too much.

"Most of my life, I've sacrificed. It's like my default setting and survival mode. I don't want it to be that way. I want to love you and keep my daughter and sister safe. I must learn to let go and let God do what He has always done. God always takes care of His children. I may or may not be Ezekiel All's daughter, but I'm God's child, and I'll trust Him to protect me."

Theory felt a tear escape. He caressed her pink-hued cheeks. "Virtuous, you have no idea how valuable and precious you truly are. Baby, you have the heart of a warrior, and I love you. We're going make it through this storm, maybe a little weaker, but much stronger in God and each other. I'm with you, baby, and God is, too, even to the ends of the age. You're His. No matter what, God will always treasure you, want you, love you and protect you. That's what Fathers do," Theory told her, though his heart was beating out of his chest. Ezekiel All was Big EZ. That might be a problem, but no matter what, he wasn't leaving or losing Proverbs.

Later that night, Theory and Virtuous were sitting on the couch, watching the movie. It was one that Theory had never seen, but Virtuous seemed to know all the dialogue. Apparently, Gugu Mbatha-

Raw was one of her favorite actresses, and she had all the movies the woman had ever done, none of which he had never seen.

Theory smiled down as Virtuous rested her head over his heart. Chauncory rested to his right, and Tory was laid up on his chest, too. Cutie had wrapped herself around his legs, drooling, but he did not care. He liked the idea of being a family man. Maybe because his family was so broken. He really did love each one of them. He could get used to this.

"I love you, Proverbs."

"I love you, too." He smiled as he ran his hand through her unbound hair. He leaned over to kiss her temple. Before more could happen, the doorbell rang.

They both let out a groan but were relieved when Jason jogged downstairs to answer the door.

"Uncle Norman, what are you doing here?" Jason asked, surprised.

"I came to check on y'all. Who does that truck belong to?" Norman questioned.

"My friend's. We're all good here. The girls are asleep, so we'll see you at church tomorrow."

"Did you at least call your dad? He was feeling really hurt that he hadn't heard from you all."

"Mamaw kept us updated, and we texted him."

"Call him, Jay. I don't understand this generation thinking a text message is a sufficient form of communication. Check on him. He wants to hear the voices of his children, not read texts."

"Yes, sir."

"Well, I guess I'll go. Tell the girls I came by. You all come eat at the house tomorrow. Tell Virtuous that her little friend needs to go home. I don't care if she's eighteen. They better not be in her bedroom."

Theory, hearing all of this and being far from a coward, was more than willing to speak to Norman. The only reason he was still sitting was because he had four people on his body and did not want to disturb them. However, he did have permission to be here. He called Mrs. Hartford himself.

Prying the tiny bodies off of him, he sauntered toward the front door to face Norman. "Hello, sir."

Norman looked at him and shook his outstretched hand. He had dark hair that was graying on the side and strong European features and hawk-like blue eyes.

"I was going to leave in an hour, which is how long Mrs. Hartford told me I could stay this evening. I have not now nor will I in the future go to Virtuous' bedroom unless I receive permission to do so. We're just watching a movie, and the children are asleep, but you are more than welcome to join us."

"That won't be necessary, but how about you come to our church tomorrow? Come eat at my house, too. I'd like to get to know you better."

"Absolutely," Theory agreed.

Then the two said their goodbyes.

Jason chuckled once Norman was gone. "You're a real charmer, Theory."

Theory shrugged his shoulders. "I fear no man, but I would never disrespect your grandparents by sneaking into their home. That's just rude, and I was raised better than that. It looks like I'll be hanging with y'all tomorrow. I should be heading out."

"Right now?" Virtuous asked, pouting.

"You better stop looking cute like that. I need to get Chauncory home anyway. We'll spend tomorrow together, maybe take the kids somewhere, too."

"Okay, love you."

"Love you more." He winked then turned to walk toward his car.

CHAPTER 10

Theory could not sleep because his mind was busy, plus, Chauncory had awakened around three a.m., vomiting everywhere. Probably because he ate his weight in cupcakes.

Even before that occurrence, Theory was restless because he was worried. It was not about attending Proverbs' uncle's church but about Ezekiel being Valor and Virtuous' biological father. What really kept him from sleeping were the repercussions that would ensue when EZ learned who his daughter was in a relationship with. It never failed that an unresolved past returned to haunt the present.

Theory did not remember much about that night, but he did learn that the victim was Ezekiel's lady. EZ was not the forgiving type. *What if that woman was the mother of Valor and Virtuous? What if he robbed their biological mother? Would Virtuous still love him? Would Valor still respect him? Would Ezekiel want to take his life?* He was sure the answer to that last question was yes.

Shaking off the thoughts, he put on his house shoes and eased out of his bedroom. He did not want to wake his son. He had a tough night, and Theory wanted him to rest as much as possible. It did not look like they were going to church in the morning.

When he made it to the kitchen, with the intention of going out the back door to chill outside with Logic, he found Valor.

Val was sitting at the table, drinking bottled water and eating fudge Oreos. That boy loved Oreos all his life. They were the only sweets that Theory ever saw him eat, and he didn't share, not even with Chauncory.

"What're you doing up?"

Valor lifted his red-rimmed eyes and answered, "I couldn't sleep, and you were making a lot of noise. I'm guessing you can't sleep either."

Theory nodded. "I got to tell you something, and I don't know if you'll forgive me."

"I know you and my sister got into an argument. We're twins; I feel things. She told me y'all made up. It's not my business. I love both of y'all."

"That's not it."

Valor paused, mid-chew, and glanced up at Theory. "What is it?"

"Proverbs told me about Ezekiel calling her; you know that's Big EZ right?"

At that revelation, Valor's mouth fell wide open, showcasing the Oreo residue on his teeth and tongue. "What? Are you sure?"

"Do an internet search. His picture and his charges will show up. Your possible biological father is Big EZ, and I think that lady I robbed back then might've been your biological mother. I'm sorry Valor."

Valor leaned back in his seat, thinking. A rainbow of colors etched his face. followed by a myriad of emotions. "Let me get my Surface Book and look this dude up." Valor padded out and came back five minutes later with his computer and powered it up.

He quickly typed in Ezekiel's name and clicked on Images. "Dude, no; not him. He's the plug; like, he was pushing big in Anderson and Atlanta." Valor looked up at Theory pitifully. "If this is our father then we owe you an apology. That man has been slanging his entire life. The dealer that gave you to Grammy was working for him. From my end, nothing has changed. You're still my brother. I still love you, and your past is *your past*. You paid for your mistake. I won't make you pay for it again and neither would Virtuous. If that's why you can't sleep, then be at rest."

Theory shook his head in awe. "There's something unique about you and Proverbs. The level of forgiveness in y'alls heart is something I aspire to have, for real."

Valor shrugged, and then he got a mischievous look on his face. "There's a blessing here. Ezekiel will end Greg. If he finds out that Virtuous is being abused by him, then you can best believe Greg will come up missing. Big EZ got an army of loyal soldiers," Valor added.

Theory had not even considered that possibility. "I never thought about that."

"Yeah. The idea that Big EZ is my dad is bothersome on every level. So, let me run something by you. And yes, I'm changing the subject."

Theory just chuckled and pulled out a chair to sit down. His long leg spread out like a V as he leaned over to give Valor his full attention. "What's on your mind?"

"I really want to go to the United States Naval Academy to play football and get my degree, but that's all the way in Annapolis, Maryland. That means I won't see you all as much. I just got my sister back and have a niece, you, Chauncory, and Gerald. Gerald said if I go, he'll also relocate and pay all my expenses. Then what about Grammy? She'll be an empty-nester. She just had that mini-stroke. I'd feel selfish for leaving her behind. Then there's my sister. I know you got her, but as her brother, her twin, I don't want her to think I'm abandoning her, you know?"

Theory let out a sigh. "Have you prayed about it?"

"Yeah, I have. I'm going to visit the campus next week, just to get a feel for it. Gerald offered to come as well. Right now, that's where I want to go. It's a great school and a great opportunity for someone like me. We've been through a lot. I lost two sets of parents, and to overcome that get in a school as prestigious as the United States Naval Academy is a great accomplishment. I want to show Tory and Chauncory that anything is possible. I've worked really hard, but at the same time, I don't want to appear selfish."

"Do what God tells you to do. It seems to me that He is leading you to the U.S. Naval Academy. We'll come visit. Don't worry about anything else; just live your life and do great. It's never selfish to go where God leads."

Valor smiled. "What about you? I know you got your SAT scores back."

"I almost forgot. I scored in the top percentile. I applied to schools in North Carolina and Georgia. If I attend school in Georgia, I'll be able to let Chauncory see his mom and sisters. I have to see who has the best engineering and business programs as well as who offers the best financial aid package."

Valor nodded, impressed. "I'm so proud of you. That's all Grammy and Pop ever wanted, for us to accomplish our dreams. If this doesn't prove how good God is, and that He is real, then nothing does. Two abandoned boys grew into men, by the love and prayer of a grandmother who refused to let us ever fail. Now, we're going to college. That's an awesome testimony."

"It is. Hey, Proverbs' uncle invited me to their church tomorrow, but with Chauncory being sick, I don't know if we'll make it. If we do, will you come, too?"

"I'm there. I hope Chauncory feels better. I know he loves some church."

"Yes, that he does. The ladies at the church love him. My son is only five and got ladies checking for him."

Valor threw his head back, cackling. "It's the Campbell way."

"For sure."

A & Ω

Tossing and turning, Virtuous gave up on sleep. She woke up Jason and told him to look out for the girls. She was headed to Greg's house. Her mind had been plagued ever since Ezekiel told her that it was Addison who had contacted him. She wanted to see if there was anything that could link the two. Addison kept some papers in the attic, and she needed to get them before Addison did. Something in Virtuous' mind told her something important lingered there.

This was the best time to do it since Greg was out of town. Jason did not like the idea but finally gave in. It was their house, so it wasn't like she was doing anything wrong. She jumped into her SUV and made the drive to Greg's house. Seeing nothing out of place, she headed to the door.

Letting herself in, she quickly locked the door behind her, stopped for a moment, and looked around the house. It had been awhile since she lived here, but it did not feel like home, and she did not miss this place. There were far too many bad memories. Shaking her head, she jogged up the first set of stairs and then the second set that led to the attic.

It did not take her long to find what she was looking for. The box was sitting in the corner, and she grabbed it and took off the top. She started to look through the contents of the unmarked box and found a journal. Normally, she would never pry into someone's personal thoughts, but Addison had long lost her respect.

Virtuous flipped through, reading random passages until something caught her eye. Apparently, Addison did not like Valerie because she blamed her for splitting up the family. Addison's father had an affair with *the help*. That woman gave birth to Valerie and left her to be raised by Addison's parents. Virtuous shook her head but put the

69

journal in her purse and kept digging. She found what looked like medical and legal documents and then stumbled upon her birth certificate, the original one that had Valerie Leigh listed as the mother. Leigh was Addison's maiden name, and Valerie was Addison's sister, the same sister born out of an affair. At that moment it all made sense, sort of.

"Addison is my aunt?" Virtuous questioned aloud, feeling her heart splinter. It was one thing to think that Addison was no blood relation to her and allowed Greg to hurt her but to be her aunt? An actual blood relative? Maybe Addison hated her, too, because she was Valerie's child. Maybe all this abuse was because she couldn't get to Valerie. It was just jealousy and hate. She was making the daughter pay for the sins of the mother. That grieved and disturbed her.

Virtuous kept on searching and found newspaper clippings about Valerie Leigh being found dead of a heart attack caused by an overdose. Tears fell from her eyes. Valerie was beautiful. She looked nothing like Addison. Body trembling, Virtuous decided to take the entire box. She would get answers. On her way out, she nearly tripped over another box that was slightly hidden. At first sight, she thought to leave it, but something told her it might prove to be important, so she grabbed it, too.

Taking a deep breath, she exited the house, locking it back up, and jumped into her SUV. Her sight was blinded by tears, by the betrayal, and by the deception of it all.

A & Ω

Virtuous' body lay splayed and unmoving on her queen size bed. Her toned frame was covered in red blotches, which was a physical sign of just how stressed and upset she was over the ordeal. Her mind completely fogged up after what she had discovered. There were a billion unanswered questions that tortured her young mind, that made her want to reach out to Ezekiel All to see if he could fill in the blanks.

Virtuous let out a long, harsh breath. So, Addison was not only her legal guardian but also her biological aunt. Addison knew that from the beginning and refused to protect Virtuous from Greg's sexual advances. Without permission, plump, clear tears roamed down her cheeks as the realization of it all threatened to destroy her.

Five minutes later, she reached for her Bible but prayed before opening it. Her heart was not in the right place to receive the message God had in store for her. She needed to clear her mind first.

It was funny how one discovery could make her spiritually unbalanced. All that progress was slowly being chipped away due to the lies and inactions of others. Closing her eyes, she said a wordless prayer. This entire situation was straining her faith. She told Theory she'd embrace faith over fear, but she felt like fear was about to defeat her.

There was no way she would be able to attend church with Theory today. Doing so would only cause more pressure, and she could tolerate no more. Her entire body, mind, and soul were fragile and fatigued. She needed rest, the kind that only God could provide.

"Sis, are you okay? Can I come in?" Jason's muffled voice came from the other side of her closed door.

Inhaling deeply, she found her voice and replied, "Come in."

A second later, his large body entered her room. His face held concern. "Vivi, what's the matter?"

"I found some interesting information. Stuff I need to share with Theory and Valor, but I'm so tired of everything."

Jason frowned. "You're making me nervous."

Shaking her head, she calmed her stressed features. There was no reason to upset Jason, though this information was important to him as well. "Sorry, where are the girls?"

"In their room watching Disney Jr. I was about to get them some breakfast when I thought I heard you crying. What's going on?"

Virtuous nodded for him to sit down so she could share her discovery. "Addison is my biological aunt, so, you and I are actually blood cousins. I found my original birth certificate. It clearly shows that my biological mom is Valerie Amelia Leigh. I don't even know her, nor do I recall Addison speaking about her." Virtuous sighed before continuing. "However, what I don't understand is what happened to her. Valor and I weren't given up until we were toddlers. So I wonder if she kept us?"

Jason nearly fell out of the chair. "What? Why? I don't get it."

"Me neither, but my supposed biological father reached out to me because Addison went to see him and let him know that Valor and I weren't aborted. All I can think is that she's trying to get back at Greg, but I don't know how Ezekiel plays into her game. I aim to find out."

Jason shook his head in disbelief. "Evil. I used to feel sorry for her. I thought she was a victim like the rest of us. A victim of Greg's madness but the more I pray and read the Bible, the more I see she and Greg are the same. We're just their pawns in their game. It stops now. No way will Maddison or Tory ever grow up like that."

Virtuous nodded her head in agreement. It was all bewildering, though. It seemed this entire ordeal stemmed from hate and anger then jealousy and now, revenge. None of it would end well for Greg or Addison.

Just as Jason was about to reply, Virtuous' cell started blowing up. She looked down and saw that it was Theory.

"Hello?" her soft voice answered, and Jason mouthed he was going to feed the girls, leaving her alone.

"Babe, I can't make it to church. Chauncory has a fever and has been vomiting since around three this morning. So, Grammy and I are staying home with him, but Valor can come."

Virtuous silently thanked God that she would not have to take Theory to church, but she hated that his son was sick. "I understand. I'm not going today either. There's just too much going on. I just want to talk to God alone and not be in a packed church."

Theory was silent; just when it was about to get awkward, he finally spoke. "You don't sound right. What's going on? My little man is sick, but you're welcomed to come here."

Letting out a sigh, she told him about going to Greg's house and what she unearthed.

"You went to that house alone?" Theory fussed.

Virtuous sensed that he was about to get all worked up, and she did not need him to do that. "Theory, don't focus on that; focus on what I found."

"Essentially, Addison, your legal guardian, is your biological aunt, and your biological mother is a woman named Valerie Leigh. I'm guessing, by the tone of your voice, this information has taken a toll on you."

"It has."

"Why don't you and the girls come over. I'll call your uncle and explain why we can't attend. I don't want you home alone, and I don't want you worrying. We'll get through this together. I promise."

CHAPTER 11

The past few days had been hectic and trying. Theory and Virtuous had not been able to spend quality time like they needed since both of their households were in chaos. Then there was the DNA test that Valor and Virtuous had taken to confirm if Ezekiel was their father. Lastly, there was the ever-looming Greg who apparently caught an infection and had to remain hospitalized a little longer.

Greg was a problem. He was not just a problem for Virtuous but also for Theory. Even in his absence, Greg was present, and Theory needed him gone. Until then, he was doing his best to be the man Virtuous and the girls needed.

Theory planned an outing at *Pump It Up* on Southport Commerce Boulevard that would allow the kids to have some recreational bonding time. Theory was even about to get his sister Cordy. Thank goodness, Chauncory had overcome his stomach issues.

Theory had to shake his head at it all. When he was released from juvie, he thought his only concerns would be staying out of trouble, finding a job, and getting into school; however, his world rapidly changed. His mindset matured, though, once he met Virtuous, his Proverbs. "Theo, come here," Valor called out, interrupting Theory's mental planning.

Theory pulled himself out of his reverie and hollered to Valor that he was coming.

Once he arrived in the living room, he saw that Valor was texting on his iPhone. "What's up? You sounded urgent."

"It is urgent! Big EZ is my biological father. You were right," Valor admitted crestfallen, his eyes as wide as saucers.

Temporarily, Theory was stunned silent, not so much at the news, but at Valor's reaction to it. It was obvious that he was unprepared for this outcome, even though they all knew it was more than a fifty percent chance.

"Allow him an opportunity to explain. The visitation form was submitted, and you're approved to see him. If now is too soon, then wait until school is out for the holiday. Once you meet him, get a feel for him and then decide what you want to do next."

Valor glanced over at Theory as if he was not expecting Theory to offer that kind of advice. "I tell you what; I'll go see him if you give Uncle Stanley another shot," Valor offered.

Theory nearly sucked his teeth and rolled his eyes, like Cutie when she did not get her way, but he refrained. "Well, in that case, I guess you won't ever know your daddy," Theory snapped and turned away a bit peeved. Besides, he had to meet with Deacon Hayes who was probably going to suggest the same thing.

"I guess not then," Valor added and stomped out, following the path Theory had moments ago abandoned.

For some reason, that hit Theory harder than it should have. Valor was not that kind of guy. He was always the first to forgive, to love, to be a peacekeeper. It was baffling that he was refusing to give his biological father a chance, especially when he willingly embraced the adoptive father who had abandoned him. It left Theory feeling odd and, well, responsible.

Before leaving the house, Theory turned back around and sauntered back over to Valor. "Val, my situation is different than yours. I personally think you should see Big EZ, at least he wants you. I know Virtuous is going to go because she has a lot of questions; at least be there for her on an emotional level. Furthermore, what's between me and Stanley is just that, between us. That's two decades of hurt, betrayal, and lies to unbury, and it won't be easy. I know that eventually, I must deal with him, but not you or anyone else is going to make me. When the time is right, it'll be right.

I have to go visit Deacon Hayes. We can talk later or not; it's up to you. Either way, I love you and will support whatever decision you make. Just don't punish a man who may have turned his life around like I did. I'm not that same dude, and maybe, your dad isn't either. Remember, he didn't abandon you; he thought you were never born," Theory replied and made his exit from the house and headed to church.

"Maybe your dad changed, too," Valor mumbled, but Theory was too far gone to hear.

A & Ω

Staci was a ball of nerves and had been ever since Penelope had confessed what she did. She could have easily phoned the police when the woman overdosed and gotten her help instead of watching her have a heart attack. All of that to get a man. Staci was virtually like her, and if she kept this information to herself then she would be just like Penelope.

If that was not bad enough, the police might pursue charges against Nocturnal because of the accident. In his current condition, he was a threat to no one. Still, the state of Georgia could charge him with first-degree vehicular homicide because of Congo's death, reckless driving, and fleeing from the police. He was looking at some serious time if charged and convicted. That scared Staci because if he was locked up, what would that mean for their children? He needed to be in their lives. He was always an active father and the idea of losing his freedom and his family was too much.

Never did she want her life to play out like this. She prayed often and hard. It seemed like she was stuck in a never-ending trial, but the light in what seemed like endless darkness was that her daughter was improving. Selma may have some developmental delays and would most likely be intellectually and physically disabled, but she was alive, and she was strong, and Staci thanked God for that.

"Staci, are you going to call him?" Jedidiah asked with a concerning look on his face. Probably because she had tuned out everything around her.

Staci had come to him and confessed everything. Jedidiah had advised her to tell the truth, especially after how she kept Chauncory a secret for so long. Here she was, in Jedidiah's office, staring at her cell phone trying to find the courage to tell the truth.

"What if—"

"No, Staci, you're not going to do that," he scolded, shaking his head. There was a bit of irritation in his voice, which was a first for her, but she knew he was correct.

"We don't live in a world of *what if* but in a *God is*. Call Theory and be honest because the longer you keep quiet, the worse it'll be. He doesn't deserve that. I mean it, Staci. If you want to free yourself, you have to be honest."

Staci nodded. It was time to do the right thing. Theory may not react well, but he had to know that he had not committed a crime. The only thing he did wrong that night was trusted the wrong people and love the wrong woman. Theory truly was innocent. All his issues stemmed from one insecure woman who would do anything to keep her man. Just as Staci had done. It was tragic the lengths they had gone through to keep a man.

A & Ω

Theory parked his truck at the church and made his way to the on-campus family center that housed the counseling offices. Just as he entered, his cell phone started to go off. Thinking it was Valor, he picked up without looking at the ID. "Yo."

"Vic, I mean, Theory. I need to speak with you if you're available." Staci's voice hummed on the other side.

Theory mentally berated himself for not paying attention. He really did not want to talk to Staci. Her entire existence annoyed his soul because he knew what kind of person she was. They had not had a heart-to-heart about what she had done, and Theory thought he was over it. But hearing her voice brought it all back. "I can't drive to Atlanta."

"I can come to you. I need to come up to Anderson anyway, but I can meet you somewhere in Spartanburg. It'll be later, but I have some troubling information that I just received, and I need to tell you." Her voice was shaky, which alarmed him.

Theory leaned his head back. He did not need any more issues. He was already overflowing with troubling information. "Just tell me because I have an appointment right now."

Theory heard an aggravated sigh leave her lips. "Okay, but just know that I was willing to tell you this in person instead of over the phone."

"Just speak Staci because you're getting on my nerves. I've had a rough one so far, so don't escalate this. I'm not in the mood, and you really don't want to upset any more than you already have," he fumed, causing other visitors in the hall to look at him.

"Sorry. Anyway, Penelope reached out to me, and she told me that Big EZ's kids, something about twins, are alive, and I was like, great, but she said it wasn't good."

"What? I'm not understanding why this is my business," he asked, frowning. Nobody better be coming for Virtuous or Valor because of his past transgressions. He did not even think Penelope was that stupid, but then again, she thought she was bad back in the day. That eased once Big EZ got locked up, but she still had Nocturnal and Congo to fall back on. Now, one was dead and the other was out of commission.

"She's the reason that the twins' mother overdosed and died. It was her, never you. Penelope set you up to take her fall. Apparently, she got you drugged, something about seeing if you were down for the crew. Well, you never even robbed the lady; she just made it look like you did. Still, I feel like she did not give me all of the story; like, there should be more, but that was all she said. I don't know the specific details, but she confessed that to me. She might come after me; in fact, she pretty much threatened me, but I've betrayed you enough times, and I just couldn't keep this to myself."

Theory almost threw his phone. His mind was saying, *For real God? Like, that's how you do me?* He felt weak, even faint. Was this woman telling him it was all a lie? He was set up by Noc's sister Penelope; was Noc in on it too? Did he set him up to ensure he was the one who got with Staci? That seemed like something he would do. Their entire family was foul. Why had he ever wanted to be part of that crew?

"Theory?"

"Staci, did Nocturnal have something to do with this? Was this his way of ensuring that he got you and I didn't?"

"I don't think so."

"He knew. Nothing occurred back then without his knowledge. It smells of him. They stole my life, so he could get you, and now, Penelope is threatening my family?"

"What? No, she would never threaten Chauncory. I really don't think Noc knew anything. She just wanted to ensure that she got Ezekiel and the other woman didn't."

"Nah, I'm reading this right. For the record, I'm talking about Valor and Virtuous, not my son. The twins that belong to Ezekiel are my brother Valor as he was adopted by my uncle, and Virtuous is my girl. You know, the one you called 'white girl'. That's me. So, if Petty Penny is coming for them then she's coming for me. I don't play about mine!" he growled.

There was silence, and Theory would have thought she hung up except he could hear her raspy breathing.

"Oh. I had no idea, and neither does she. Penelope has never met them. Please, Theory, whatever you do, don't let this get you in trouble. You have my word that on my end, I'll keep an eye out and will tell you if I hear anything. Theory, I'm so sorry; not just about this, but about everything."

Theory didn't reply. He just hung up. Yeah, good thing he was in church because he was going to need every ounce of Deacon Hayes' advice, wisdom, and prayer. Satan was really coming for him. There was a flicker of vengeance gnawing at him. He had removed Nocturnal from his list a long time ago, but now, he was back on as was Penelope. They would be seeing him very soon.

A & Ω

Nocturnal was pissed. His best friend was dead. His son was not his; half of his leg was gone, his right hand was bandaged from second-degree burns and they shaved half of his hair off for some stupid operation. He could not recall why he had surgery. Then his mother lectured him as if he was a child, and now, he was looking at felony charges. It was coming from all sides, and he had no idea what to handle first or how to handle it. That frustrated him to no end. He was Nocturnal Kershaw, fearless in the streets, untouchable. And now, he was disfigured—and helpless. Oh, how the mighty have fallen.

Here he was, about to be charged with first-degree vehicular homicide, which was a felony in Georgia. He had run-ins with the law, but they could never make anything stick. He was too slick, but now it all seemed to have caught up with him. As if knowing he was the reason that Congo was dead was not enough to make him feel worthless and guilty. Why also charge him with his death? He even tried to call Congo's mom, and she refused to accept his calls. The one who fed him, who let him sleep at her house, who treated him like a second son, didn't even want to hear his voice. That destroyed him.

If that was not bad enough, his newly hired defense attorney Devona Gateway told him he was looking at three to fifteen years in prison and that was for a first-time offender. Apparently, it was far worse for habitual offenders. That did not console his spirit. In addition to that, they would revoke his license for three-years. Not that he could drive anyway, he only had a leg and a half.

The bottom line was that he was going to do time, and charges were inevitable. The lawyer thought because of his disability, a word he hated, they might go easy and place him in the protected wing. Again, that did not bring him peace. He wanted to do no time; he wanted his best friend back, along with his leg and his hair. He just wanted a redo. That was impossible.

What was worse of all was that he would be separated from his children. They would hate him because he killed their Uncle Congo. What about Chauncey? Even if Theory was his biological father, Nocturnal was the one who raised him. That burned his soul. How could his life end like this? No son, no best friend, and no freedom, all because Staci lied for years to him, and he exploded. How was he supposed to act? He was a man with nothing to live for. And that was a dangerous place to be.

All he wanted was the best for his family, which was why he was leaving the game, but he waited too long to make his move. This entire situation had him stressing, and at times like these, he would reach out to Congo. But Congo was dead, and that still was not real to him. In his mind, his bruh was still out there, but in his heart, he knew he was gone. He never even got to say goodbye. If he had only stayed in Anderson that day, Congo would still be alive. He ended his right hand's life over something that had nothing to do with him.

Everything in him wanted to cry; his nostrils were burning; his breathing was increasing, but the tears would not formulate. Nocturnal hurt, in a way he was unable to explain. He felt deeply exposed and lonely. Both were unknown feelings, and he had no idea how to deal with them.

Turning to his side, he banged his head against the bed. This was him reaping what he sowed, all the lies, the cheating, the street-scheming; this was him getting it all back, and he could not handle it.

Tightening his fists, he let out a distressed cry, only to be halted by a knock on his door, followed by someone opening it. Nocturnal thought it was most likely the nurse. That old, tired, bird-face lady eyeing him like he was trash. She got on his nerves with her owl-like eyes and mannerisms. Old, clocking granny saw everything. The last time she eyed him, he tried to throw the bedpan at her. It missed her by an itch, but boy, did she call him everything but a child of God. They even called psych on him.

They were probably going to put him on the psych ward now because he was self-harming and tearing up his bed.

Nocturnal focused on the door and was surprised to see a man enter his room.

"Excuse me, are you Percival Kershaw?"

The guy in front of him was a stranger; however, something about the man looked familiar, but for the life of him, he could not place his face. Maybe that was due to the car wreck, too. His memory was still hazy about certain things.

"Who you? I'm Nocturnal or Noc," he explained.

The man shook his head and pulled his arms up and that was when Nocturnal noticed he had a Bible in his hand. Nocturnal suppressed a retort. God was not trying to save him. Nocturnal was the enemy, a murderer who probably broke all the commandments at least three times over. So, this was a waste. This was probably some of Staci's nonsense.

When he was out, thinking that he was dreaming or something, Staci would sit by his bed and read Bible verses to him and prayed over him. It was all pointless. He was still less of a man, all cut up and alien-like. None of that lessened the pain. If this preacher dude was coming in here to tell him all the goodness of God, he would tell him where to stick it.

Ain't no God for a goon. Nocturnal had done too much to ever be redeemed, not that he was looking to be saved. Nah, not at all. There was a reason he was given the name Nocturnal. He was a dark dude who did some evil things, and people probably thought he had no heart. So, if this man was here to save his soul, he may as well leave. Nocturnal was beyond saving.

"Hello, Nocturnal, I'm Pastor Micah Carver. I volunteer here, and I'm also the senior pastor at the church that Staci and your children attend."

Staci's old sinning self was behind this. As if God would forgive her for all her lies. Her hands were just as bloody and guilty as his.

Nocturnal still did not know the man, but the more he stared at his face, the more a name began forming in his head. It was not Micah, more like Jiffy, or Jed, or something like that. "Aye, you got a son or a relative named Jaffar, Jimmy, or Jedi?"

"Oh, you mean, Jedidiah. You two have met," he stated with a warm smile. For some reason, Nocturnal's screwed up face did not send him fleeing. The man just advanced deeper into the room, looking all-welcoming and preachy. It made Nocturnal itch.

"I caught him pushing up on Staci, using her grief and hurt to his advantage. But that's whatever 'cause he can have that fraud. I'm done with her. She's just using him. Staci can't be without a man, so you might want to warn your son. Staci's tricky. Oh, also let him know don't be playing daddy to my children. Even laid out like this, I got a crew that will move at my say so. Now, you can leave. This conversation has come to its conclusion. I didn't request for no holy man to be in my room," Nocturnal quipped.

Pastor Micah nodded but remained unmoved, which further irritated Nocturnal. This man really was trying him. "I know you did not request my presence, but God did, and I work for Him. Therefore, I need to listen to Him. Maybe you should also," he replied as he pulled a chair and sat down near Nocturnal's bed. His voice had softened, but there was sternness in his tone.

"It seems to me that you could use someone to talk to. I heard a bit of a disturbance upon my arrival. Also, I see blood seeping from your forehead. Let me call a nurse to assist you then maybe you and I can have a conversation. I'm not your enemy, Percival, and neither is Staci or Jedidiah. We're all allies and family, and the same God that saved me, can and will save you, too."

A & Ω

Theory looked at Deacon Hayes with weary eyes. He had exhausted himself after telling Deacon Hayes about everything that happened with Staci. The deacon knew about Chauncory but had no idea that Theory had been set up. This session, Theory wanted to talk about how to deal with Greg and Addison and how they could save Virtuous, yet he was still dealing with his past that wouldn't allow him to move forward.

"I know the Bible says to be angry and not sin, but everything in me wants to unleash *Vicious*. That lie took me away from my son and my family. I broke Grammy's heart. I broke my own, blaming myself for that woman's death, a woman who was Valor and Virtuous' biological mother. I still haven't told Virtuous that, but now, I don't know what to tell her because apparently, I'm completely innocent. What kind of sense of humor does God have 'cause that's foul?"

Deacon Hayes listened, and once Theory stopped talking, he ambled over to him and gently placed his left hand on Theory's broad shoulder. "Now, son, you know I treat you and Valor like my own grandchildren, no different."

Theory nodded. He had been coming over to the house more and more. He and Grammy were spending time together, and he and Valor both were okay with that. They both liked and respected Deacon Hayes. He was always one to speak his mind.

"So, let's rethink what you said. That latter part about you doing time for nothing, I'm going to disagree with you on that."

"Huh?" Theory growled, offended.

"Hold on. I didn't interrupt when you were speaking, so get that bass out of your voice and change that face. I need you to close your mouth and open your ears." He paused for a moment to make sure that Theory did as he asked. "Okay, now, when you were younger, you were all about that street life, so much so that Naomi had to put you out. I think after the loss of your grandfather, that was pretty much it.

"You lost your anchor, so you went seeking that street life, except it wasn't what you thought it would be. Then you were so lost in it that you had no clue how to get out of it. Now, what Penelope did was wrong, but don't view it as a waste; it was a blessing because I'm sure if you hadn't gone to juvie, you would have done something worse.

"Something like getting jumped into that gang, probably arrested, and on serious charges, and never see the light of day. Look at what's going on in the world today; they build those steel plantations to enslave black men, and when they can't arrest you, they kill you, even when you comply. So, son, getting arrested and sent to juvie saved your life. You finally found God. For once, there were no distractions or outside influences. You finally saw who your friends were, as well as the kind of family you have despite Stanley, but most importantly, you know your enemies.

"You could have been dead, Theory. Life could have ended much worse, but God saved you. At the end of the day, all you got is God. You'll not disrespect our Father by going back to the person you used to be. I'm not letting that happen. I'm an old man, but don't think I won't knock some sense into you. You were lost once, but we aren't about to let that happen again. You hear me?"

Theory dropped his head. He heard the truth in the words that were spoken.

Deacon Hayes had a way of breaking things down and getting to the root of the problem and daring you to try him. Truthfully, Theory was thankful for his mentor because he was sure Pop, his deceased grandfather, would have said the same thing. Plus, he would have knocked Theory upside his head. "You're right. It just tore through me, and all I wanted to do was get back at them because I know Nocturnal had a hand in it. However, I have a son that watches me, and I don't want to make a move that I wouldn't want him to make. I told Valor I would be better, and I have to be, but most of all, I never want to disrespect a God who sacrificed His son on my behalf."

Deacon Hayes smiled. "I like what I'm hearing, but words are fruitless until you put them in action.

"True."

"Oh, one more thing; have you spoken to Stanley? That last meeting was painful but also therapeutic. Maybe we can try again, this time, with level heads. He hurt you, deeply hurt you, but he's here now, and he's hurting too, Theory. Be the olive branch," Deacon Hayes advised.

Theory smirked. They were coming from all sides at him. "Not you, too. You know Valor tried that as well. He told me he would go see his bio-dad if I gave Stanley another shot. I'm not ready. As much as I respect you, Deacon Hayes, I won't be pressured into a situation I'm uncomfortable with. Maybe I'll talk to him after I visit my maternal side of the family, but I can't do Stanley right now. There are other issues I need to resolve that are far more important, issues that I have not even been able to discuss with you, but when the time is right, I'll deal with Stanley."

"I respect that. Don't wait too long; none of us knows when our time will come, so we should never put off anything we can do today. I get it, really, I do. Just know I love you and I'm here for you. Tell Valor if he needs to talk to me, I'm available. I had no idea he found his biological father."

"Will do," Theory replied and gave Deacon Hayes a man hug.

"Deacon Hayes said, "Theory, whatever those other issues are, let me know. You're too young to withstand so much on your own. Until we talk, give it to God, pray, and never stop praying. There isn't any issue in the world our Father can't get you through. Let Him. That's where we mess up; we give it go, God, then snatch it back. Before you do that, remember *Thou shall not steal.* Let God work in every aspect of your life and follow the path of faith, not fear." Then the two prayed as they always did after a session and Theory left.

83

CHAPTER 12

Greg's hard, wintery eyes glared out the window into nothing. Misery had overtaken him as he was tired of being in Utah. His mind was a mass of confusion, revenge, and fiery rage. For the first time ever, he was spending the holidays without his family. He received a call from Maddison, but that was all. His family's absence created a bitter hollowness in his heart. This was not how he planned it. A juvenile delinquent had turned his sweet, innocent Virtue against him. What's worse was that Greg never saw him coming. The entire time, he thought it was Nimo who had Virtuous' attention.

Every time he thought about Theory, which was all the time, he twitched. That nobody was destroying his perfect little world. Greg wanted him gone.

Letting out an aggravated sigh, Greg shook his head as he replayed Brad's update. Brad was one of his first successful police explorers who became a police officer. Greg had written him a letter of recommendation and was a job reference for him. That made Brad indebted to him. He would do anything Greg requested. That was why he was perfect for Greg's plan.

Brad's job was to pull Theory over, continuously, for the slightest infractions. The plan was to upset Theory enough that he would explode and get locked up or shot. What Greg had not counted on was for the man to be an ideal citizen with discipline and patience. However, that was not what caused him alarm. It was the fact that Theory had been seen around town with Tory, acting as if he was the father when Tory was *his* daughter. That would not be tolerated. This thug had taken his entire family, even Jason and Maddison, were fond of him. That made Greg hate him more. Theory's actions were infuriating and demeaning. The level of disrespect he was showing was going to cause something bad to happen.

Virtue was pushing Greg to his limit, deeper into a think-less abyss for which there was no exit. When the darkness surrounded him, deleterious things happened. Only if Virtue would get in line and be the good girl, he knew she was, this would end peacefully. Instead, she wanted to be a naughty girl and refused to recant. Her only choice now was to come home, recant, and let that boy go.

Greg Hartford would not continue to be disobeyed and disrespected. He would not be made to look a fool, and no one took what belonged to him, no one. Whatever happened next would be all her fault as Virtue was forcing his hand.

"Greg, come on and eat. No need to fume over what you can't change. You know you're innocent, baby. Your family, once they get through the shock of it all, will come around too," Sandy's annoying voice drummed through his thoughts.

Greg fought to keep the disgust from his facial expression. That was another issue he had to handle. Before, his family was on his side. They rejected the notion that *he* would ever harm anyone. Then Addison popped up.

Addison and her family, including Tommy, had called a meeting while he was occupied and dealing with Virtue's allegations. Addison had somehow swayed his family against him and in favor of herself and Virtue. She made herself a victim, but that was a lie. For her disloyalty and her lies, she would pay as well. He had it all thought out, and he would put his plan into play soon.

Addison would never have happiness, and she would never have custody, not even shared, of Maddison. Judgment day was coming, and he was the judge, jury, and executioner. A gleeful grin spread across his face as he mentally played out how he was going to eliminate all his enemies.

"Greg, honey, come and eat." Sandy's annoying voice interrupted again. Her thin arm wrapped around his shoulder as she stood, tiptoed, to run her lips across his cheek. He wished he had never started a fling with her. Virtue was right as to why he chose to do so, but now, he regretted it. Sandy was clingy and too needy. Never would she compare to Virtue. That was just another loose end he had to deal with.

A & Ω

"No! No!" Tory screamed as plump, juicy tears fell from her illuminated indigo eyes, causing Theory's heart to seize. Virtuous declared it was time for the kids to get their flu shot. Theory agreed, but now he regretted his decision.

Tory's wailing almost had him crying. Her little fists were swinging in defense, trying to stop the nurse. "Proverbs, can't you just let her get the mist?"

"No, the shot is better."

Tory's little azure eyes declared war on her mama; she quickly wiggled out of Virtuous' hold and went running to Theory.

"Da-da no, Dada!" she hollered, leaping into his arms. That was it. She had never called him anything close to "Dad" before. Hearing her say that made him want to shut the whole thing down. Theory looked over at Virtuous who shared his shock.

"Proverbs, she's not getting an injection. Just give her the mist. Y'all upsetting my baby. You got her face all red and covered in snot. There's no need to stress her like that."

Virtuous shook her head in defeat, and Theory knew he won that round. "Fine. Maggie, can she get the mist? Only Chauncory will need the shot."

At that, Chauncory whipped his head around and side-eyed Virtuous like she lost her mind. Then his rustic eyes turned to his father for help. "I'm sorry, son, but due to your age, you need the shot."

Chauncory let out a loud sigh before he balled up his lips, crossed his arms defensively, and turned his face from his daddy. Theory, being a softy when it came to the children, quickly attempted to come up with a plan that would bring a smile to his son's face.

"Hey, I'm taking you and Tory to Chick-fil-a, and I'll buy you each a toy if you take your shot like a big boy."

Chauncory's head popped up, and there was a mischievous glint in his eyes. It was clear that his little brain was working on how to get the better end of the negotiation. After a few seconds, he replied, "I need two toys Daddy, and an ice cream cone, and five dollars."

"Done."

Chauncory smiled brightly until the nurse came back and prepped his arm. Sensing his apprehension, Virtuous quickly lifted Chauncory up and placed him on her lap. She wrapped him gently in her arms and started to sing to him and gave him soft butterfly kisses. Theory's heart melted a little. Chauncory was so hypnotized by her voice that he seemed to have forgotten the shot, and when he told the nurse he was ready, it was already over.

"That wasn't so bad!" Chauncory exclaimed. A huge smile etched his face, though his eyes never left Virtuous'. All Theory could do was simper. Chauncory had a little crush on Virtuous.

Next, it was Tory's turn. The hiccup fit she had worked up was calming down. Her skin was back to its natural hue, and her face was clean. "It's your turn now, baby girl. All she's going to do is use the mist, no shot," Theory explained soothingly.

Tory nodded but had yet to release her arms from around his neck. After about three minutes of sweet talk, she finally let go. He turned her around and sat her in his lap so the nurse could administer the mist.

"Good job, Tory."

Tory smiled. "Good Dada," she cooed and kissed his cheek.

Yep, Tory officially had him wrapped around her little finger. Anything his little princess wanted; she could have. He loved this little girl. If he had his way, she would be his daughter legally very soon.

Theory looked up at Virtuous and winked.

A & Ω

Resting, Theory had his right arm behind his head, his long legs splayed in different directions on the couch. On the television was *Alvin and the Chipmunks,* a favorite of Chauncory's. Tory, who only made it through the first ten minutes, was knocked out on his chest. Just like her mama, she liked to be near his heart, or maybe, she liked to sniff him too. It did not matter because he cherished both of his ladies.

Tory's little fist gripped his button shirt as if daring him to move. Her breathing was in rhythm with his. The sweet scent of baby lotion filled the air. Her mass of honey blonde curls roamed, unbound, tickling his chin, but he refused to move her. They were pretty much inseparable.

Theory's left arm was tenderly wrapped around Tory to secure her body. His mind replayed her calling him Dada. It made him feel just as good as when Chauncory called him Daddy for the first time.

God had changed him completely. Back in the day, it was about the streets, girls, and getting money, but all he wanted now was his family. Virtuous, Chauncory and Tory were everything to him. Never in his life did he ever think he could love the way he loved them. There was nothing he would not do for them, and nothing could make him ever stop loving them.

The soft laughter from Chauncory eased him out of his reverie. Their matching rustic eyes caught each other. Chauncory wiggled his eyebrows at Theory. He was probably up to something. He and Virtuous were putting up Christmas decorations, which they had been working on since after breakfast.

A grin spread across his face as he observed Proverbs instructing Chauncory on how to put the ornaments on the tree. They had a little system going.

With a joyful heart, Theory just took in the sight. This was what he wanted—a family, a home, and security. When he was locked up, never did he dream he would be a father or in a committed relationship. He never thought he would want marriage at a young age, but this felt right. This moment was perfect.

In fact, life was great right now. Since Thanksgiving, the ordeal between the Hartford family and Virtuous had calmed down. A few days ago, Virtuous and Valor finally met some of their paternal family. It went well.

Theory and Virtuous had an amazing time in Atlanta, and Jason and Maddison were able to come also. Their presence excited Virtuous. The look on her face when they arrived at the hotel was a look that Theory wanted to see on her face all the time, which was why he had not told her about being harassed by the police.

He was constantly pulled over for any minor infraction, but instead of showing frustration or anger, he notified Montez, Tamari's father, and attorney Wentworth. Something told him that Greg was behind the harassment. Greg was probably hoping that Theory would react in anger, thereby giving an officer the right to harm him. However, Greg and his loyal followers underestimated Theory. Nothing was going to separate him from God or what he and Virtuous were building.

What really made his heart swell with pride was how much closer he and Virtuous were after just a few weeks of doing the Daniel fast and reading Psalms and Proverbs daily. They prayed together every night, and it was helping them both, in their relationship together and their relationship with God.

"What are you smiling about, Theory?"

Still smiling before responding, he took in the glow that was Virtuous. She was beautiful. "Us, our family, and how much we've grown together and in Christ in such a short period. I'm just happy."

Virtuous nodded in agreement and then leaned down to kiss him. "It feels so peaceful now. I mean, I know everything is not in order, but I feel so connected to God and to you that I feel safe. Even after the threats from Greg. I just feel covered by God. This is the first week I've slept uninterrupted and not had a nightmare. That's significant progress. I'm thankful Deacon Hayes suggested we do the Daniel fast and a devotional together. I feel mentally, physically, and spiritually healthier."

"Me too. I'm thinking about reaching out to my mom's side of the family. Maybe we can invite them to come visit for Christmas."

Virtuous' eyes shimmered with excitement. She started clapping her hands at the suggestion, which made Theory laugh.

"I like that idea. Maybe after Valor and I officially meet our Dad, we can have a huge Christmas dinner and invite my paternal side of the family. It would be a great way to end the year and start the new year."

"I agree. So, you're calling Big EZ 'Dad'?"

Virtuous blushed, but she held eye contact. In the past, she would have dropped her head, so Theory was proud to see her keep her head held high. "I won't to his face, not yet, but when I speak of him in conversation."

"Don't blush, baby. I was just teasing you. I'm impressed by the man he's turned out to be. I'm glad that he and Valor are doing better. I'm thankful that you finally get to witness what a real father is and have a great family. You deserve that."

"You do, too," she whispered in his ear, her soft breath tickling his earlobe.

"One step at a time baby. Speaking of time, what time is it?"

"Clever," Virtuous commented, letting him know that she was aware of him changing the subject. "Almost eleven-thirty."

"Well, me and the kids got to get ready. I'm taking them Christmas shopping and meeting up with the guys."

"I'll pack the kids a bag. Are you sure you guys can handle four children?"

"Babe, I got this."

"Okay, but if you need me, just call. Tamari, me, and your cousins will be doing some last-minute shopping."

"Y'all have fun 'cause me and the kids will." Then he kissed her forehead and eased up, still holding Tory.

CHAPTER 13

Nervously twiddling her fingers, Virtuous could not believe she was finally meeting her biological father. It took her about twenty minutes to decide on what to wear, causing Valor to become annoyed with her. This was a big deal. They were meeting their father for the first time. Adrenaline rushed through her marrow at the thought, and Virtuous had barely slept the night before. Her mind riddled with *what-ifs* and how Ezekiel would perceive her.

All her life, Virtuous never thought she would see the day when she would meet her real father. Fighting back tears, Virtuous recalled a conversation she had with Greg.

"Can I ask you something?"

He leaned back; the nonverbal action was his way of saying yes.

"Why?" Virtuous questioned, her soft voice barely audible and her eyes full of doubt and insecurity. At the end of the day, all she wanted was a father, not an abuser, or a lover; just a father. Why couldn't he just love her without hurting her?

"Why what, darling?" Greg asked sweetly. His wintery blue eyes gazed into hers as if the entire situation was normal.

"Why can't you be a dad to me like you are with your other three children?"

"I fell in love with you, Virtue. I didn't do it on purpose, but it happened. It's okay because you aren't my biological daughter. There's nothing wrong with us loving each other. Sometimes, stuff like that happens. You're my special girl and have been since you came to us. We've always had a unique bond."

Virtuous shivered at hearing that endearment. "But I'm your daughter, not your special girl. You and Addison are my legal guardians, and no, we don't share blood, but you're still my dad. You're the only father I've ever known. Why can't you love me without hurting me?" She was frustrated because he didn't comprehend her, and she was doing her best to fight back tears. Sucking in her the sadness, she controlled her emotions and tried another tactic. *"How would you feel if someone did to Tory or Maddison what you do to me? If a man said the same things about your biological daughters, would you feel the same way?"*

Greg frowned, but she could tell that he didn't like the question, but he also didn't like the answer.

"Well?"

"I wouldn't let it happen, but that's not us."

"Greg, I'm someone's biological daughter. Can't we just be father and daughter? I need a father, not a lover," Virtuous *implored and realized at that moment she should have stayed silent. He violently yoked her up, scaring the life out of her. "Daddy, please."*

"You're someone's daughter who didn't want you. Remember that!" he raged.

Greg was wrong, though. It appeared that Ezekiel did want her. Even though Greg had broken her body, damaged her soul, and stolen her virtue, her biological father did not abandon her. Instead, he sent for her. With trembling hands, she reached out to Valor for support. He was her calm. With Theory unable to be by her side, having her brother was the next best thing.

Virtuous noticed Valor was listless and reserved. He knew Ezekiel as Big EZ the criminal. Because of their father's past, Valor blamed Ezekiel for Theory losing his parents; whereas, Theory blamed his parents for their own behavior. Who Ezekiel used to be was a long time ago, and everyone deserved a chance to do the right thing. It seemed Ezekiel wanted that chance. However, proving that to Valor was near impossible. He had about as much hostility against the man, as Theory had against Stanley, and that worried her.

Melancholy etched through Virtuous as the idea of her brother and Ezekiel not getting along. She quickly removed that feeling as her brother's soft baritone interrupted her private musings.

"There he is."

Virtuous looked in the direction that Valor was glowering, and her eyes spotted him. Her breath halted as she took him in, and her pulse began to quicken. This man was her father. It gave her chills. The little girl in her that she thought died long ago wanted to jump out of her chair and hug him. The little girl she never got to be wanted to know what a real father's touch felt like. She longed for it like rain during a drought. The little girl in her wanted to hear the sweet musings a father whispered into his daughter's ear as he jovially hugged her after a long day at work. Would he understand that need or think her silly for even having such thoughts? How sad it was that Theory wanted nothing to do with his father, yet she wanted everything from a man she only had spoken to briefly.

Holding his gaze, Virtuous took her father in. Ezekiel was at least six feet four inches and well-built with tattoos peeking from his state-issued uniform. However, he carried himself in a way that commanded respect. He had the presence of a CEO. It was as if he had the ability to attract people to him. Ezekiel possessed that charming glint in his eyes that gave off the perception of safety but also of power. Even in total silence, he emitted dominance and strength. This man was fearless. This man was her father. If only she could borrow his clout, she could defeat Greg.

Like a sharp-eyed eagle, he surveyed his surroundings before turning his attention to them. Then he did something she did not think possible—he smiled. It changed his entire appearance, so much so that it elicited a smile of her own. They favored him; the chin and ears were spot-on; his hair, however, was more ginger than honey blonde. Even though they were strangers, she felt like she belonged to this man. She had a father, a father who wanted her—*maybe*.

Valor squeezed her hand harder as if he felt what she was feeling. His touch momentarily diverted her attention away from their father and back to him. When Virtuous looked over at her brother, she noticed that he had a mean mug that gave Ezekiel a run for his money. It was apparent that her brother did not like this man, and that baffled her.

Ezekiel sat his large body down, completely unaffected by Valor's unwelcoming greeting. Instead, he focused his intense gaze on them. It was as if he was imprinting them into his mind.

If anyone were watching it from the outside, it was probably creepy; however, this man was meeting, for the first time, the children he thought were dead. Of course, it was overwhelming. The moment was spine-tingling but also pleasant. Instantly, Virtuous felt safe in his presence. That was huge.

"Hello, I'm Virtuous, and this is Valor."

Ezekiel grinned. A soft chuckle escaped his thick lips, showcasing his white teeth. "I figured that out. I'm just in awe that you two actually exist. Thank you for coming. Your mother named you well. I've read up on you both, and I'm so proud of the people you've become." His voice sounded like woven thread. His speech was neat and well-articulated. For some reason, she had imagined something different.

Valor let out a sigh at the latter statement, which caught Ezekiel's attention. "Are you okay?" He sounded genuinely concerned. Even Virtuous was worried. This was not the brother she knew.

Valor just stared quietly at him.

"Valor!" Virtuous chastised.

"What? I told you I would come, but I never said I would talk to him. He's a drug dealer. He feeds that death to his own people. His crew nearly destroyed Theory's life, and now what? You want me to be all *Will Smith, Just the Two Of Us*? Not happening. I'm just here for moral support and your safety." Then he side-eyed Ezekiel as if daring him to speak.

Virtuous felt heat swim up to her cheeks. She was unprepared for Valor's outburst and a little embarrassed. "No, but you can be nice. He's still our father. It's not his fault we were separated, and we all have a past Valor. Is it right to judge him? It's not like he does that anymore. Let's just talk and give him a chance. Please."

Valor nodded, but he turned his head.

"I'm sorry sir; he doesn't mean it. Grammy raised him better than what he is currently displaying."

Ezekiel lifted his brow as if he disagreed, though there was a bit of amusement in his eyes. Even with Valor being so rude, Ezekiel did not seem to be offended. "You don't have to call me sir."

"Well, I thought it disrespectful to address you as Ezekiel or Big EZ. Mr. All sounds like a business deal. It's too soon to call you 'Dad'. I, mean, you are. However, I wouldn't presume you'd care to be addressed that way either. So, 'sir' seemed the best option."

"Call me whatever makes you comfortable." He gave her a reassuring smile.

Virtuous nodded. There was an awkward silence before Ezekiel spoke again. "Who is Theory?"

Valor snapped his head back and glared at him. His entire face frowned as if he was offended by the question. "You probably know him as Vicious."

Ezekiel's face wrinkled in confusion, but then a look of knowing spread on his face, "Angel's boy? How do you know them?"

"Angela," Valor corrected before continuing. "I was adopted by Sherry and Gerald."

"What?" Ezekiel questioned, his large body leaning back as if he was floored by the information. "That's interesting."

"Yeah, so I know all about you and your lifestyle," Valor replied snidely.

"How did you two even meet then?" Ezekiel asked, completely dismissing Valor's attitude. His ability to do so awed Virtuous.

Virtuous explained as quickly as possible, and Ezekiel hung on her every word. He gave her his full attention, and his reaction to her didn't make her feel uncomfortable as it would have if she were speaking to Greg.

"Well, tell me this; since you're eighteen now, are you away from that guy who was abusing you?"

Virtuous dropped her head. It was not as easy to speak on as everyone thought it was, especially to strangers. There was still a lot of shame and guilt she was dealing with.

"Baby girl, don't you ever drop your head. You have nothing to be ashamed of. I need to know about this man— everything about him. Addison never came back to see me. She dropped the bomb and then disappeared. That has eaten at my soul since I found out. My daughter is being abused had I known you were even alive; you would've been with my family and none of this would have happened."

Virtuous nodded, and a little piece of her was elated that he cared so much.

"If Addison's smart, she won't ever come back to see you. I'm guessing you and your lawyer haven't spoken recently. If you had, you would know that Addison is just as guilty and as abusive as Greg. It was all on the news when she attacked my sister at the daycare," Valor revealed.

Ezekiel's eyes went cold and Virtuous stilled. That was the part of him that Valor must have known. She physically felt the frost. Greg would not stand a chance against Ezekiel. For the first time, Virtuous saw and felt what it was like to have a father who cared for her. Greg wanted to control and abuse her. Ezekiel seemed to want to comfort and protect her.

"It's okay. Addison hasn't contacted me, and Greg isn't coming back until next week. He has an infection from his gunshot wound.

He's recovering in Utah. My daughter and I are fine at our grandparents' house."

"Virtuous, I'm your father, and I don't want you or my granddaughter around that man or his family. Those people aren't your blood, they are his. I'm sure if you stay, they'll protect him and not you. So, you're moving out. I'm sure my lawyer is working on it. His firm deals with family law as well. Now, my wife Penelope knows I want you all taken care of until my release next year. Until then, Nadel Wentworth can set you up in your spot. I got it covered. I'm so sorry for the years I've missed," he paused as emotions took over.

Valor lifted a brow at his admission, and Virtuous patted her brother's hand.

"I'm so serious when I say I never knew you existed. Valerie told me she was having an abortion. I didn't want that. I never even suggested that. It was her father who got into her head. Your mother was so sweet and meek. You have some of her qualities, Virtuous. I had to remind her to keep her head up, too. Her father was hard on her. He's what you'd call verbally abusive. He never hit her, but his words cut her deeply. I'm so sorry I let you get hurt like that."

It was a tender moment that Virtuous was sure she would remember forever. Everything that Ezekiel said she believed. It was obvious that he was just as tortured as she was. "It's alright. I know you feel bad, but I don't blame you. I did but that was before I knew the truth. I'm sure Addison had a hand in this somehow. Neither she nor Greg holds power over me, and I'm going to go to the authorities and tell the truth."

Valor looked over at his sister. "For real? I've been wanting you to do that since I found out."

"It's time."

Ezekiel smiled. "Anything y'all need let Wentworth know, and it'll be done. Be safe Virtuous, please. I have some people who'll look out for you. Even though I'm locked up, I'm here for you both. I love y'all so much. I hope y'all will come to see me again." Next, he turned his attention to his son. "Valor, I get it. I understand your anger. Back in the day, I was not a good man, but the man I am now is different. Please forgive who I was, and I hope one day you can accept who I am now."

Valor nodded; the only show of emotion was his red face. Virtuous smiled and offered Ezekiel a hug before they left the visitation room.

A & Ω

Greg was distressed. Addison had set him up, and he never saw it coming. Greg had no idea that Virtuous was Addison's biological niece, and now, Tommy Leigh wanted to threaten him. That did not stop his feelings for Virtue, however; the plan was still the same. Though Tommy and Addison thought they were going to block his plans, he was going to block their plans.

Hearing the footfalls of Sandy and his brother who had just arrived last night, Greg quickly changed his demeanor. He was certain that Virtue would never turn on him; he had her completely brainwashed.

"Greg, how're you feeling? Think you'll be ready to leave tomorrow?"

Greg did not reply. Instead, his eyes got watery, and his skin reddened as his emotions got the better of him. "I can't believe this."

A worried Sandy and a perplexed Norman glanced at each other before returning their attention to Greg. "Greg, what's up? I thought the doctors cleared you," Norman finally spoke.

"They did, and it's not that. I, uh, well, when I was in the hospital, I got a visitor. It was Addison's father Tommy Leigh. He told me that Virtue is his biological grandchild, which I never knew. Her biological mother was Valerie, which is probably how Addison got custody of Virtuous so fast. She never told me or Virtuous that. It was bad enough she attacked our daughter, but Virtuous is her niece, our niece. To add insult to injury, she told Tommy that I've been…" Before he could finish, he started to cry, causing Sandy to leap into action.

"Baby, what?" she cried, smothering him with caressing hands and comforting coos. It nerved him to no end, but he played it up.

"Why keep that lie about Virtuous, and why involve Tommy? Is this about the divorce?" Norman asked.

Greg nodded and then collected himself and gently pushed Sandy away. "Addison lied and told her father that I've been sexually abusing Virtuous. He threatened me. Seriously, why would I violate my own daughter? I mean, I never adopted her but I'm legally responsible and I would never harm her. Tommy believes Addison. I just don't know what to do. I've been worried ever since he came, thinking he might kidnap the children or even try and turn Virtuous against me. I can't get into contact with her. I'm just so tired of Addison coming for my family and my livelihood."

Norman sighed and shook his head. "Sandy, can you leave us, please?"

Sandy started to refuse his request, but Greg stopped her. There was no reason for her to be part of the conversation. She heard what he wanted her to hear, so now, she could go busy herself doing something else.

"Okay, well, I guess I'll go cook something." And then she was gone.

Greg turned his wet eyes back to his brother. "Addison is just determined to get a rise out of me. I'm doing my best to remain calm, but to accuse me of sexually assaulting Virtue? Just the accusation alone, though untrue, could ruin my reputation. That's what she wants."

"Greg, no one would believe her. It's absurd and we all know it. She's reaching because she's desperate," Norman reassured.

"It hurts, Norm; it hurts that she would take it this far."

"I know, but you'll be done with her soon, and she's only digging her own grave."

Greg nodded but remained quiet in thought for a moment before asking, "What's Virtue up to? Is she okay? Are you sure Addison hasn't gotten to her?"

"I'm sure. She and her friends are shopping for the Winter Ball dance, I think Cate said. Cate is helping with decorating the whole thing. From what I can tell, she's busy with her art project, her new friends, and some guy."

Greg nearly shot out of the bed. Sweat started forming on his skin. He felt his breathing become labored. *She would not,* he thought to himself. Virtuous was not that stupid. "What guy? Nimo? Virtuous knows my rules about no dating and no boyfriends. I want her focused on school."

"Calm down. She's eighteen. I think it's okay for her to have guy friends. We know she's a responsible teen. No, it's not Nimo; he's dating another girl. This guy Virtuous hangs with doesn't attend her school. He seems to be a nice Christian guy from what I hear. Plus, when I met him, he was quite respectful. Everyone adores him; our parents, your daughters, Jay and Cary," Norman explained.

Greg shook his head as anger pulsated through his body. He was sure his blood pressure had risen to stroke levels. He had been gone for almost three weeks, and in his absence, Virtuous had lost her mind. That was okay. He was going to help her find it, and whoever this guy was would pay for touching what belonged to him.

"Greg?"

"What, Norman? Do you think I care about your opinion on how I raised my daughter? She's impressionable and could be in danger. I'm pissed, okay? I leave my child with my family, and you let her loose. Now that we know she has Addison's blood flowing in her veins, that means we have to tighten the reins, not ease the grip. I can't believe my own parents let this mess happen," Greg ripped into his brother before calming down enough to ask, "Who is he? I need a name, so I can do a background check on him." Greg was losing it. Montez was right. Virtuous was sneaking behind his back.

"No Greg." Norman shook his head. "Let that girl have this. After everything she's suffered this year, let her have moments of happiness. Don't be that dad. If the guy was bad news, I would be with you all the way, but let this go. You have bigger issues with Addison and Tommy. Focus on that and let Virtuous enjoy her life. She deserves as many happy moments as she can get. Besides, things with The Leighs are about to get ugly."

Everything in Greg wanted to punch his brother, but two things held him back; his health because he was still weak and the fact that Norman was right about this issue with The Leighs getting ugly. In fact, things were going to get deadly. There was no way he would ever let it be known that he was sexually assaulting Virtuous. Ever.

CHAPTER 14

Virtuous rested in Theory's embrace. Untamed strands rested on his gray t-shirt as he gently ran his fingers through her hair. Eyes closed and body at rest, Virtuous recounted what happened when she met Ezekiel and how excited she was about it. Theory patiently listened and assured her that better memories were coming to her.

The couple was sitting outside as a cool breeze combed over their exposed skin. Virtuous inhaled the Carolina air mixed with Theory's aura. Her body nestled deeper into Theory's warm chest as she listened to the beating of his heart. It was her favorite melody.

After such an exhausting couple of days, it felt like home to be in Theory's arms. When they were together like this, nothing else mattered.

Exhaling a calm breath, Virtuous listened to the outside serenade of chirping chickadees. Night was close behind as the moon started to reveal itself. Peaceful moments such as these were what she lived for. Silently she prayed that there would be more moments like this. Prior to meeting Theory, she had no idea this kind of peace existed.

"What are you thinking about?" Theory's cajoled. His smooth, contralto voice interrupting her thoughts.

Virtuous simpered at the sound of his voice. It coated her like an electric blanket. After all, they had been through, it just felt good to be together. "About the future since I finally feel like I have one."

Just as the words left her lips, Theory's hand caressed the side of her face. "Yeah, me, too. When I got out of juvie, I never would have dreamed I'd meet somebody like you. I didn't even know young women like you existed. Besides, the last thing I wanted was to be in a relationship. I trusted no one outside of a few family members. After Staci's betrayal, trusting anyone was difficult. Not to mention, I felt odd and off. Like, I was removed from society for six years, and the idea of assimilating was terrifying. Then my mind told me that no one wanted a man who had a past like mine."

This time, Virtuous caressed him and gently tugged on his chin. "I thank God daily that He chose me for you. When you entered my life, I could see clearer. You showed me that a person can go through horrible beginnings and still survive and have a life after the pain.

"I was faltering in my faith and living in fear until I met you. Then all this good stuff started happening. From you, I found Valor and my biological father, and that's so cool. I'm forever thankful. I'm looking forward to Thanksgiving and Christmas this year because I have a real family now. I've never had that before."

Theory beamed as he toyed with her hair. "Yeah, me, too. That'll be my first time celebrating the holidays with my family—and you. I'm looking forward to making better memories together," Theory replied. "I, mean, I'm somebody's daddy. I have a whole little mini-me, and Tory, she's mine, too. God keeps on blessing me, and I'm also forever thankful." He paused for a moment, causing Virtuous to look up at him. There was a humble look on his face, and his eyes were slightly misty.

"I lost a lot, Proverbs. When I first got locked up, I thought I lost everything. I felt like Job, except I didn't have his faith or patience. I was more of a runner like Jonah and a bit of a doubter like Thomas, but now…now, I know *He is* who He says He is. God provided for me while I was on the inside, and then He entrusted me with a son, my family, my health, and my Proverbs. I'm overflowing in blessings. I never thought I would be. It's humbling. I never thought I would ever care, cherish, or love someone the way I do you. That's how I know that we're going to be alright."

Virtuous could not hide her smile but fought to keep her tears at bay. "You say the sweetest words. I'm glad that you care, cherish, and love me because, before you, no one else did. I love you, Theory."

For a moment, they just relaxed in the quietude of the night, glancing at each other from time-to-time, but simply appreciating being together. Just as Virtuous was about to close her eyes, she remembered she needed to ask him something.

"Will you go to my Winter Ball with me? I would have asked earlier, but with everything going on, I forgot."

"Of course. I never got to go to any dances or the prom, so I'm game."

"That's right. Well, I'll make sure that you have the best time."

"I always do with you."

A & Ω

Theory entered the hospital in Atlanta. After the night he had with Virtuous, there was no way he was letting his past harm her. After a long prayer, Theory knew it was time to deal with Nocturnal. Now, he was handling business. He and Nocturnal needed to have a face-to-face and quash whatever issues Noc had with him.

Clearing his mind, Theory ambled into Nocturnal's hospital room and pulled up short. He had no idea what he expected to see, but it was not this. Nocturnal looked different: frail, aged, and weak.

"Vicious? Whatchu here for? Come to gloat about Chauncey being yours?" he asked crudely.

He might have looked different physically, but he still had the same rude attitude. "Nah. I'm too old for that ignorance, but I appreciate you taking care of my son. However, what I came here to talk about is your sister."

A bemused frown clouded Nocturnal's face. "What about her? Cos, she knew you was Chauncey's she father and didn't even tell me. I ain't dealing with her," he grumbled, the sting leaving his voice.

Theory shook his head. Penelope was vile, for real. "Look, your sister confessed that she set me up. It was she who did the robbery that I did time for. I was drugged, and she put the gun and loot on me. Then a few days later, she overdosed Valerie. She did so to solidify her hold on Big EZ. When this was told to me, I knew you had something to do with it. I'm here to tell you this: Big EZ is the father of Valor and my girl Virtuous. If your sister comes for them in any way, there will be major problems. No one comes for my girl, my brother, or my son and gets away with it."

Nocturnal's tired eyes stared, perplexed, at Theory's. That stunned Theory. It seemed that what Theory was telling him was unknown to him. "Whatchu talkin' 'bout? They be having me on some serious medication. So, run that by me again. I'm confused."

Theory sighed and went through the story again. "Your sister murdered the mother of Virtuous and Valor to secure a man. Now that Ezekiel is aware that his children from Valerie are alive, I believe your sister might try something. Let her know it won't go down like that."

"Murder? Man, I ain't have nothing to do with setting you up or that lady. Yeah, I was messing with Staci, but honestly, my level of cocky wouldn't allow me to stoop to that level. No way would I set you up to keep her. I had money, power, and women scheming for me. I had no need to come for you. On everything, Penelope never told me 'bout any of that. I just thought you wanted to be down and that was why you did it. I can't believe she did that. Does EZ know?"

Theory shook his head. "He needs to know. Your sister should tell him, but I don't trust her. I have a meeting set up with his attorney to let him know. I don't do secrets and lies. No one is messing with my family."

"Agreed. I feel you on that. Um, how Chauncey doing?"

"He's adjusting well. I brought him down here with me. He's visiting his sisters. I can bring him to see you if you want."

"You'd do that for me?" he questioned incredulously. It looked like some of the life that drained from him was coming back.

Theory shrugged his shoulders and took a seat in the recliner. "Look, Noc, I spent a lot of my life being angry and holding grudges, and it got me in trouble. Now I appreciate every gift God gives me. Whatever was between us is long in the past. I believe you when you say that you weren't in on Penelope's scheme. I'm done with what happened back in the day. Like I said, I appreciate you taking care of Chauncory.

"You should be in his life also. I'm not trying to take him away from you and Staci. He loves you, and I'm not going to be that guy. I learned something from Valor. He has an adoptive dad and his bio-dad, and I see him struggle with how to interact with them both. He feels if he accepts one then he can't accept the other, and that's not true. I see it like this; my girl and I love Chauncory, you and Staci love him as well. It's not about biologicals and non-biologicals; it's about us working as a unit to create the best Chauncory we can. He needs all of us for that."

Theory watched as Noc's eyes watered, which shocked him. "You always were a deep brother. You're a real one, Vicious. I apologize for how I treated you in the past." Noc paused for a moment as if he were collecting his thoughts. "I told Congo you was intelligent and a leader, which made me paranoid. You're a good dude. I'm glad Chauncey got your DNA and not mine. I appreciate you letting me be in his life. I need my kids because losing Congo and facing double-digit felony time got me all pressed, stressed, and depressed."

"I feel ya. I was there. It was juvie and not the pen, but I was there. I'll pray for you, man."

Nocturnal smirked. "You'll pray for me? You sound like that holy man that visits me every day. I tell him don't come back, but he comes anyway. He told me he doesn't answer to me; he answers to God. I told him ain't no God for a goon."

Theory shook his head. That was classic Nocturnal. "You're wrong about that, Noc. I can see you're not prepared to receive Him right now. You're buried under fear, guilt, regret, discouragement, and anger. It's eating away at you. Until you let that go, nothing else can come in. You're blocking your blessings, my G.

"I didn't come to preach to you, but I'll share a little wisdom. It's got to be tough to deal with all that loss, not just of your best friend or your kids, but your body and livelihood. Here's what is; you're still alive. God saved you for a reason. He left you behind to be a blessing, not a burden. Be thankful and grateful for that," Theory told him and paused for a moment to let it all sink in before adding, "And Nora's pregnant."

Nocturnal's eyes grew large with fear. "It's not yours; at least she says it isn't, so be calm. I don't want you going into shock or nothing. She's giving the baby to Ms. Willamina because she's not ready to be a mother. Just like your children need you, I'm sure Congo's son or daughter will need you. So, if you can't get right for yourself, then do it for your children and Congo's baby," Theory advised before getting up from the recliner, stretching out his long, toned body. Then he stared Nocturnal in his eyes and said, "Just so you know, God loves goons, too. He loves me, and He's changed me. All you need to do is let go and be open to receiving Him. Chauncory and I will swing by later, and I'll bring you some Arby's. That's still your favorite, right?"

Nocturnal smirked. "Yeah, Theory, that's my favorite. Just don't let Nurse Ami see you bring it in. She hates me with a passion."

Theory nodded and left.

CHAPTER 15

Theory and Chauncory were headed back to Spartanburg after spending half the day in Atlanta. His son had talked his ear off until he talked himself to sleep. Now that it was quiet, Theory had time to reflect on the day. All he could do was smile and praise God.

The way Theory and Nocturnal interacted today let him know that God was indeed working in him. Theory was prepared for the situation to go left; he foresaw anger, bitter words, false accusation, and a fight, but there was none of that.

Sure, he and Nocturnal were not bosom buddies and probably never would be. They were men, and they could conduct themselves in a manner that would create a wholesome and welcoming environment for Chauncory. He even had a cordial conversation with Staci.

Theory looked over at his son, and a small smile spread across his face. For his son, there was nothing he would not do. Sending a quick prayer of thanks, Theory turned down the road that led to Grammy's house. By August of next year, he planned to be in school and in his own place, and, possibly, engaged to Virtuous. That would be perfect.

As Theory turned into the driveway, he quickly noticed that Stanley's sedan was parked to the far right. A cold prickle cascaded up and down his arm, but he calmed himself. If Theory could deal with Nocturnal, then he could deal with Stanley.

Letting out a deep breath, he parked his truck and picked up his son before exiting the vehicle. Slowly, he trekked up the steps and onto the porch, the entire time mumbling to himself to be serene and not reactionary.

Unlocking the door, he cautiously entered the house and found Stanley standing up, holding a sleeping Cordy while talking to Grammy. It seemed their conversation was concluding. It came to a complete stop once Theory entered the house.

Grammy noticed Theory first and then Stanley turned to see what had caught her attention. A quick look that Theory could not decipher flashed across Stanley's face before he regained control.

"How did it go?" Grammy asked.

"Chauncory enjoyed seeing his family. I took him to see Noc as well. It's safe to say that Nocturnal and I have dealt with our issue and respect each other as men and fathers," Theory replied.

There was a twinkle in Grammy's eyes. "That was really mature of you, Theory. I'm proud of how you are handling this new dynamic. My baby is growing up into a fine man."

"As you know, Deacon Hayes doesn't take it easy on me. You raised me right, besides there isn't much I wouldn't do for Chauncory. Besides, Noc has lost a lot: a best friend, half his leg, potentially, his freedom, a son, and his daughter is still fighting for her life in NICU. That man needed something to hope for, you know?"

Grammy nodded in understanding.

"Where's Valor?"

"He and Gerald went out. I believe to see a movie and then to eat. Valor's going to tell him about Ezekiel." Grammy replied.

"Oh. Well, y'all excuse me. I need to put this boy down. All the cupcakes he gets Proverbs to bake him are adding up," Theory teased as he made his way of the room and into his bedroom. As soon as he got his son settled, he felt a presence in his room and instinctively knew that it was Stanley. The two had not interacted since the major blowout that had occurred in Theory's bedroom weeks ago.

Closing his eyes, Theory mentally counted to ten before standing up and turning around to face Stanley. The two, nearly identical in looks except Stanley was growing a beard and had age lines around his eyes, just stared at each other.

"I, uh. I just wanted to say hey. We haven't spoken since the last epic blowup. I just wanted to tell you that I love you. I appreciate you being honest with me and that I received your words. I can't make up for the past, but I would like, when you're ready, to build a relationship with you.

"My addiction caused me to be neglectful and abusive to you, and for that, I'm truly sorry. I was sick. I am sick—my addiction is a sickness. I understand that now. That's not an excuse. It's just the truth. I failed you as a father, but I'm here when you're ready to receive me. I'm going to stay here. Apostle Amos helped me get a job, and Cordy's attending the daycare at the church. I found a counselor here as well. I'm building a good support system. I even reconnected with some friends back in Anderson. Not my drug buddies; most of them are dead anyway."

Inhaling and exhaling a deep breath, Stanley stood as still as a statue, waiting for what Theory assumed to be a response. However, before anything could be said, Virtuous' ringtone shattered the quiet, and Theory quickly answered.

"Proverbs," Theory greeted excitedly, but that excitement quickly died down when he heard what sounded like shouting and screaming.

Theory's entire body froze. "Proverbs…Virtuous, baby can you hear me?!" he shouted, still not getting a response.

Without a second thought, Theory shot by Stanley and headed for the front door. "Grammy, call that cop friend of yours. Proverbs is in trouble. I think Greg came back. Contact Valor as well; he knows were to come."

"Let me come with you," Stanley requested.

"C'mon."

A & Ω

The scent of fear mixed with tears and sweat permeated Virtuous' bedroom. She was not expecting Greg until tomorrow. She and the girls were taken by surprise when he arrived. Somehow, he found out about Theory. Greg did not know his name, but he knew that he existed, and he was livid. First came the verbal assault. Greg launched degrading words and slurs at her with the impact of an atomic bomb. Then came the threat of violence.

Greg had torn through the house like a Category 5 hurricane. He was like a man possessed. Virtuous had Tory and Maddison huddled behind her, both terrified and crying. Virtuous was nearly as scared as they were. She knew exactly what Greg was capable of, which was anything.

Stupidly, Virtuous allowed herself to become lulled into a false sense of security and peace. Nadel Wentworth was able to contact Serena, and Virtuous told her that she was ready to talk and needed Serena's assistance. That had all happened earlier in the day, and Serena promised that she was on her way back to the states. Having that knowledge, Virtuous started thinking of life without Greg, but that was a mistake. She never factored in Greg finding out about Theory.

Again, Virtuous was at Greg's mercy, doing her best to keep her faith intact when fear was all that she felt.

"Look at me, Virtue; you look at me when I talk to you!" Greg roared, causing Virtuous to jump out of her reverie.

Obeying his command, she glared at him. He was a sight. Greg's skin was a ferocious red from the anger that had consumed him. Saliva spewed from his thin lips and dripped down his chin. He looked deranged. Obviously, he was not a hundred percent healed after the gunshot incident or the infection that followed, but he was strong enough to overpower Virtuous.

Greg's eyes were a stormy, violent blue that made her shiver each time she glanced into them. They spoke of the evil he was and prepared to inflict. This felt like déjà vu when Greg had attacked Addison, beating her with his bat and pulling out his firearm. Trying to think of a way to get the girls to safety, Virtuous eased her cell phone to Maddison.

Prior to this, Virtuous had taught Maddison how to use the phone, and who to call. She knew to dial 9-1-1 and then Theory. With all this going on, she was not sure if Maddison would remember the plan, but she prayed silently that the little girl would. Their lives depended on it.

Why had LeAnn and Neman left for the night? Where was Jason? Why did she wait this long to seek out help?

"Who is he, Virtue? How long have you been lying to me?"

Deflecting his attention Virtuous stood up on shaky legs. "He's just a friend, Greg, okay."

"No, he's your boyfriend. I told you that you belong to me. You think because you're eighteen that what? You run something?" he spewed as he aggressively stumbled toward her.

Virtuous didn't run. God did not give her a spirit of fear, she mumbled to herself as Greg violently pushed her. The power of his physical assault caused her back to crash into the desk and propelled her forward. Excruciating spasms sliced through her body like cold ice, but she would not yield. Greg was her Goliath, and he would be defeated.

Enraged, Greg grabbed her again and slapped her so hard that the hearing in her right ear went numb and quiet. Her sight had become hazy. Hot tears streamed down her heart-shaped face, but she was not going to falter. She had to fight back. She had to fight for her sister, for her daughter, for their survival. God promised her plans to give her a future and hope, and she was claiming it, claiming everything Greg said she could not have: a real father, untainted love, family, freedom, and her virtue. It would be restored. Greg had taken enough. She would not give him more.

Building her strength and feeling as if she had the support of an army behind her, she glared at Greg. Absorbing all the past and present torture and channeling it, she let out a warrior cry and charged Greg, causing them both to tumble. Then she fought for every year he stole, for every sick game he played, for every memory he mocked. She punched, kicked, clawed, and screamed until her breathing became labored until her arms were nothing but limp, liquid noodles. It physically hurt to breathe or blink. He would not win. Her body was hers to give and not his to take. It ended now.

Seconds felt like forever as her hearing was assaulted by coughing and the frantic thumping of her heart. Was this death, or was death still lingering like a vulture? Matthew 11:28 echoed in her mind. *Come to Me, all you who labor and are heavy laden, and I will give you rest.*

Off in the distance, she could hear whimpering from Maddison and Tory, their little voices pleading for help that she could not give, seeking safety her battered body could not offer. That broke her heart. Every inch of her fought to move so she could comfort the girls, but her body did not adhere to the command. Instead, it fought against her just as hard as Greg had. Tears drowned her face as she choked on her saliva. *"Please God, don't..."* That was all she could manage to choke out.

Virtuous' mind went swirling all her hopes and dreams, past and present, and a future she may never have clashed violently. Barely conscious, the smell of copper attacked her nostrils, and she wondered how much damage Greg had done to her and if she had done any to him.

Closing her eyes, she started to mentally pray but soon felt a presence over her. Adrenaline surged through her, and she started fighting again, but her powerless punches only connected to air. "No!" she shouted. That one word took more energy than it should have, but she reached for the last bit of energy she had left to end this battle. Death may come to her, but it would come to him also.

"Stop, Proverbs, I'm here baby. You're safe. Stanley got the girls. It's okay. I'm not going to hurt you. It's me. It's Theory," he cooed softly.

"Theory?" Her body immediately relaxed. *Safe,* her mind reassured her. God sent Theory to save her. Comfort surrounded her instantly at his presence.

"Yeah, it's me," he soothed, drawing her back to the present.

"He knows, and he was going to…"

"Shush, save your energy and don't worry, baby. Greg's going down," Theory vowed as she gently lifted her fragile body into his arms. His tears mingled with hers, And Virtuous wanted to soothe him but moving felt impossible.

"I ache all over. I think everything is broken."

"I'm going to take you to the hospital. He won't ever hurt you again Virtuous; not you, Cutie, or Tory."

"You promise?"

"Absolutely."

"I'm tired. I just want to sleep. So tired."

"Stay awake for me, Proverbs; you might have a concussion."

"'Kay. Don't let me go. Don't leave me."

"I'll never let you go, and I'll never leave you. We're forever and always."

"Forever and always," she repeated.

A & Ω

"Did they arrest him? Where is he?" Valor asked in rapid succession, his eyes burning with anger. His body had been quaking with unrest ever since his arrival. There was nothing anyone, including Theory, could do to calm him.

The hospital quickly filled with the Campbell family, but the Hartford clan had yet to arrive, except for Jason. Theory was pacing as he just finished recounting the story of what happened.

It was unfortunate that the time they arrived; Proverbs had beaten Greg up. Theory really wanted a piece of him. He was able to kick Greg and punched him. He would have done more than that, but Stanley stopped him.

Tory and Maddison's screams nearly undid him. He never seen two children more terrorized. Those girls should have never witnessed that attack.

"Nah, that serpent crawled out of that like a champ. No wonder Virtuous was scared to tell anyone about her abuse," Theory snapped, eyes blistering with anger and regret.

"Calm down, Theory. I know you're upset, but she needs you to be tranquil so she can relax," Stanley advised and attempted to place a resting hand on Theory's shoulder. "She's been through enough, and the last thing she needs is to see you upset. It'll trigger her, so try not to allow your anger to prevail."

Theory turned his stygian eyes on Stanley and quickly shook the man's hand off him. "Did you not see what he did to her? She was bleeding from her head; her face was swollen; she was fighting for her life and for Maddison and Tory. I can't un-see what that coward did to her. I'm not angry. I'm enraged. Not only that, those police officers thought I was the perpetrator," Theory fussed before getting up from the seat he was sitting in and started pacing again. This waiting patiently was for the birds. He needed an update.

Those dumb cops automatically assumed, not asked but assumed, that the black men were guilty. All because they knew Greg. Never in his life had he ever had a gun drawn on him until tonight. It was a blessing they did not shoot first and ask questions later. Theory was sure they could have if it had not been for Cutie and Montez. He and Stanley would have been in the hospital as patients, in the county as prisoners, or in the morgue as corpses.

Right now, he felt trapped and desperately wanted to see Virtuous. His soul needed to be reassured that she was safe and doing well. If he could see her and hear her voice that would ease the pounding of his heart and the pulsating headache that was claiming him.

"I agree the police mishandled the situation, but they didn't know the story at the time," Stanley added, causing Theory to nearly jump out of his skin. He had forgotten that Stanley was present. Seemingly, Stanley missed it all and continued to talk. "Theory, being enraged won't help Virtuous. Listen to me; you've done extremely well for yourself considering your start in life. Don't let this one moment be what takes you back. Be angry but do not sin, right? Isn't that what the Bible says?"

Before Theory could reply, Jason snapped. It was just a room full of tension and everyone was on edge, but Jason was boiling. "I want to kill him. He waited until I was gone, and he attacked my sisters!"

Jason bellowed, causing the entire waiting room to go still. Even the television seemed to go quiet.

"Jay!" Maisha warned.

"What? He could've killed my sisters. I have the right to express myself." Maisha just rolled her eyes and crossed her arms.

Theory covered his ears, not wanting to hear anyone say anything. He needed silence to think clearly. All he felt was guilt.

Guilt riddled his body like bullet wounds. It tore his soul into pieces to see Virtuous laid out like that. It was clear she had nothing left in her, but she was willing to fight until her last breath. She was fighting for her life and for her sister and daughter. Eighteen. She was just eighteen, and here she was fighting a man who was supposed to love her and protect her. She was so terrified that she did not even recognize Theory, her heart. "I let her down," he mumbled, stopping mid-stride.

Maybe if he had not spent half the day in Atlanta this would not have happened. Maybe he could have saved Cutie and Tory from witnessing such a traumatic event. How many times had he witnessed his parents fight each other? Domestic violence and sexual violence did not just affect the victim; it impacted the witnesses also. Theory never wanted the girls to ever encounter anything like that.

Taking a deep breath, Theory shoved the memories back before they overtook him. After this, he was going to need to talk to Deacon Hayes or he might explode again.

"What's going on? What happened to the girls?" Norman questioned, with Cate and Cary behind him. Their frantic facial expressions showcased their concern. However, Theory did not acknowledge their presence. A part of him wondered where they had been since what happened had been hours ago. Had they gone to see Greg first? Right now, they were not important, and he let Jay handle his own family. Theory's only concern was the girls and Virtuous.

Feeling a pair of eyes on him, Theory glanced over at Valor, and they spoke without words. Both made their exit to find out where Virtuous was and to talk to her before Greg's family could. If it were up to Theory, they would not be allowed to see her. He blamed them, too. No way were they that clueless.

As the pair exited the waiting room, they ran into Nadel Wentworth. Theory looked over at Valor. He knew he hadn't phoned Wentworth.

"I called him. I thought Virtuous might need some representation, and I knew he could also get into contact with Ezekiel," Valor explained.

"They didn't arrest him or if they did, he only stayed like two seconds. I'm sure I saw him being put into the other ambulance. You know them fools thought I had attacked Proverbs and Greg?" Theory growled.

"I know, but we'll get him. Virtuous did a good job of documenting her abuse. Jason has given a statement. We can get a conviction. He can cry his innocence, but the evidence is mounting. The fact that he is the biological father of her daughter, well…look guys, I can see the hunger for vengeance in both your eyes. Don't do anything. Leave everything up to the county solicitor who, believe me, will take this case forward."

"Cool, but we're going to see her now, and I don't want anyone to bother her. Also, can you draft some paperwork to make sure that Virtuous has full custody of Tory? I'm not sure if they'll let her have Maddison, but I don't want any of them in the custody of Greg or Addison Hartford," Valor added.

"It'll be done. Go check on Virtuous. I'll be here for as long as necessary. I'll contact Ezekiel immediately to update him."

CHAPTER 16

It was Virtuous' second day in the hospital, and her body still felt the aftermath of Greg's assault. She was extremely exhausted from both the physical trauma and whatever they used to medicate her, but at least she was alive. As soon as her eyes opened, she prayed to God. It was all Him that saved her life.

As she turned to retrieve her Bible that Theory left for her, the door to her room swung opened and Mamaw LeAnn entered. There was something about her appearance that caused Virtuous hesitation. Unsure of how this interaction would conclude, Virtuous discreetly observed her.

"Virtuous, honey, we couldn't see you yesterday. We tried, but some lawyer wouldn't let us. I'm here now. Well, I just want to know what happened. Did Theory do this to you?"

The tired feeling was now completely gone. Instantly a surge of heat shot through Virtuous' body. The idea that Theory could ever hurt her was extremely offensive. "Theory has never hurt me. He's been doing his best to protect me from Greg," Virtuous wheezed out. The machine monitoring her vitals started to buzz loudly. She was sure her blood pressure and heart rate were increasing.

"What?"

"Your son Greg is abusive—physically, psychologically, and sexually. I never told anyone because I knew no one would believe me. He's a cop with white male privilege and a savior complex. People adore him. He's a family man, and supposedly, a man of God. No way he'd be an abusive pedophile. Like, even now, you're fighting between believing me or Greg. Right? How dare you insinuate that Theory could ever be violent towards me? He's the reason I've survived this long."

"Honey, Theory has a violent juvenile record. He practically murdered someone. To call your father that word is hurtful."

"Hurtful is telling lies on Theory, not telling the truth on Greg," Virtuous hissed.

At the inflection and anger in Virtuous' voice, LeAnn looked down at her hands, her skin turning several shades of red, but her mouth didn't open.

Calming herself, Virtuous continued, "Greg is Tory's father."

"Of course, he is. I know for a fact that he would never hurt Tory, Maddison, or you. He loves you Virtuous. Is this because you know he does not approve of you dating?"

"You know for a fact, huh?" Virtuous laughed but it soon turned into a hacking cough. Once she got it, she replied, "He's Tory's father, and I'm Tory's mother. Addison never had a child. After Maddison, she was unable to. When he got me pregnant, they both devised a plan. They falsified the medical records, and you all fell for it. As soon as I started to show at seven months, I was pulled out of school to give birth to your son's daughter. I was never sick. Greg's sick!"

LeAnn shook her head as if that just did not make any sense. "That's enough. Don't speak so about your father. Understand that we're not mad. Greg can be a bit controlling, and I understand you want your freedom but don't tear apart our family. This has Addison and Tommy written all over it. They're making you lie. You know Greg loves you; we all do. This can be forgiven and forgotten."

Hot tears prickled at Virtuous' eyelids, but she was not surprised. People always wanted to re-victimize the victim, make them think that it was somehow their fault. Never would any of this be forgotten, and forgiveness was a long way off. She would not lie to save family pride. Lies had made her suffer far too long, and there would be no more suffering from her to preserve this family's reputation.

Sighing heavily, Virtuous knew for sure that this would be the last time she dealt with LeAnn. Greg was her son, her blood, and Virtuous was nothing to this woman. It hurt, but she knew there would be emotional casualties in this battle. That was okay. Virtuous had her brothers, her daughter, Theory and his family, and no need for the Hartford family. Inner peace had entered her heart because God knew the truth, and He would keep her and protect her.

"Bye, LeAnn. I appreciate the kindness you bestowed upon me until this point. The truth is your son violated my body and my spirit for years, and Addison let him." Taking a cleansing breath, she continued, "Please don't come back. I need support that you can't provide. Anything else you need, please direct to my attorney."

Virtuous spoke boldly, apparently upsetting and confusing LeAnn, but she dabbed her wet eyes and exited the room without looking back.

That action said everything. Even though Virtuous stayed silent for years to avoid this moment, she was glad it was over. The sting was not as bad as she thought it would be. They had their season, and Virtuous could not shed a tear for that. Their rejection was for her protection.

A & Ω

After a few more days in the hospital, several stitches, a concussion, and some minor bruises later, Virtuous had finally been released. Prior to her discharge, Neman attempted to visit her. By that time, Theory provided a list of people to the hospital staff who could see her, and none of the Hartford family was on it. It was later discovered that LeAnn had snuck onto her room.

Even days later, the interaction with LeAnn still plagued her. There were anger and hurt feelings, claims that Theory was trying to divide the family and control Virtuous—all lies. Theory's main concern was always for her. That was why Virtuous agreed to everything that he did to ensure her protection. At eighteen, she had control over who she chose to act on her behalf, and that was Theory.

All Virtuous wanted now was to be done with the situation and move on with her life. Would that ever happen? The truth was out now and there would consequences. Those consequences could negatively impact the new life she desperately sought.

Serena assisted her in finding a safe place to stay. Serena had a friend that help relocate survivors of abuse. The apartment Virtuous was in was well secured. It was unsafe for her to live in a shelter because Greg, being a police officer, knew or could find out where the domestic violence shelters were. They had to place her somewhere he did not know about.

Days after her hospital release, Wentworth was able to help her get a permanent order of protection. Since she and Greg shared a child together, that also allowed her full custody of Tory. Thankfully, her school was willing to work with her on her assignments, and her senior art project was still on schedule.

Now, Addison and her family were also claiming that Greg was abusive to all the children and that she should have full custody of

Maddison. Ironically, Addison attempted to visit Virtuous, along with her father Tommy in the hospital, even though, months ago, she had attacked Virtuous similarly.

For now, Greg was placed on administrative leave with pay. At least, Virtuous would not have to see him at school. Maddison was staying with LeAnn and Neman, but Jason was there to keep an eye on things. Virtuous knew that Maddison was safe. Any interaction Greg had with Maddison had to be supervised at his request. Even now, he was doing his best to be manipulative. People were already taking sides, and most were for Greg.

However, the one issue that bothered Virtuous and kept her up at night was not that people thought she was a liar but Greg himself. With the way the situation was going, Greg had to know that she had given her statement to the police about the abuse and that he fathered her child. Although releasing the truth was enduring and empowering, it also endangered her. He would surely retaliate.

In the past, that fear allowed Greg to maintain control over her, but she was no longer that person. Today was proof of that. With only a week left in school before Thanksgiving break, she was back. She was a little nervous, but her resiliency and faith would not allow her to cower.

Before, fear made her want to do things that faith told her was not aligned with God. Then she remembered a passage that Theory sent to her. Isaiah 43:1 "*Don't fear, for I have redeemed you; I have called you by name; you are Mine.*" Just this morning before she drove to school, the scripture John 14:27 popped up on her Bible App. "*Peace I leave with you. My peace I give to you; not as the world gives do, I give to you. Let not your heart be troubled, neither let it be afraid.*" Virtuous meditated on that verse repeatedly until she had it memorized.

It was that verse that helped her to decide, after all, she had suffered, that coming to school this morning was the right decision. After parking her SUV, Virtuous mumbled a prayer, and then she gathered her belongings. Just before she exited her vehicle, her cell phone dinged to let her know she had a message. Virtuous glanced at it and smiled.

My Heart: *Remember Isaiah 43:1 that you are God's and that I love you. Have a great day beautiful!*

Virtuous: *Thank you & I love U!*

After sending the message, Virtuous looked up and saw Tamari. She was glowing in a gold dress, arms outstretched with a big welcoming smile on her face. Virtuous quickly embraced her. It was like they had not seen each other in years when in reality, Tamari had come and stayed with her several times in the hospital.

"I started not to come. The school said I didn't have to be here. Then I read John 14, and I knew it was time to bury my fear and live by faith."

"That's my girl! I'm glad you did come. You know you're my *shero*. There's no reason for you to hide because you did nothing wrong. Daddy and I fully support you. He said he knew something wasn't right, but once everything happened, he understood it all. We're in this together. Anyone says anything out of the way, let me know. I got you."

"Thanks, Mari. I'm really thankful for you and your dad's support."

"That's what best friends and future sisters-in-law do," she cooed, wiggling her eyebrows and causing Virtuous to laugh. Tamari was not giving up on her quest to snag Valor. For some reason, that lifted her spirit. That felt good; she had not laughed in a while.

Tamari's confidence had a positive impact on her.

A & Ω

By lunchtime, Virtuous was sure that none of her fellow students cared or maybe they did not know about Greg attacking her, but no one said anything. That was a blessing. Some of the staff gave her pitiful, knowing glances, but no one commented on anything to her.

Tamari and Virtuous headed to their regular table, and the guys were already there. Virtuous hesitated when Cary looked up at her but let out a relieved breath when he smiled. For some reason, she thought he would be angry with her. Only Jason and Maddison could see her in the hospital, even though Norman, Cate, and Cary had come by.

"Hey guys," Virtuous greeted calmly, testing the waters.

Cary's eyes never left hers. The smile was no longer plastered on his face, and she could tell that he was just as cautious as her. Probably wondering what she was thinking and how this interaction was going to go. She was thinking the same.

Cary spoke before she did. "I'm sorry." It was simple but also full of emotion. Cary was the clown of the group; he liked to tease, so hearing him say "I'm sorry" and meaning it was a bit of a shock, but he had nothing to apologize for, just like she did not. No, this was all Greg; he was at fault.

"I won't accept your apology because there's no need to apologize. It's not on you," Virtuous replied, ignoring the confused looks of Nimo and Kasen.

"But—"

"It's okay, Cary, really. Thank you for offering."

A small smile rested on his face. Just like that, the moment was over, and they started chatting about the Winter Ball. While they were lost in their conversation, Virtuous started thinking about everything. She wondered had the police arrested Greg yet. What would be the side effects of her finally breaking Greg's rules? Would he come for her or even Theory? Would he blame Jason?

Deep in thought, Virtuous didn't notice Sandy until the guidance counselor was in her face. Her lips were moving, but Virtuous had no idea what she was saying.

"Ma'am?"

"I need you to come to my office," Sandy stated politely.

Virtuous' eyes widen in confusion. The request was odd. Why would Sandy want to talk to her? And about what? Unable to sleep the night before, Virtuous finally finished her college and scholarship applications. There was no way it had anything to do with that. Plus, Virtuous never sought Sandy out for assistance on anything. She always sought guidance from her art teacher.

"Virtuous?"

Nodding that she was coming, Virtuous grabbed her backpack, gave Tamari an iffy look, and proceeded to follow Sandy.

A million thoughts ran through her mind. For some reason, Virtuous felt like this was a set-up. Like, as soon as she entered the office, Greg would jump out at her or something. What if this was a kidnapping plot?

Okay, maybe her mind was being overactive, but since being released from the hospital, sleep had eluded her. Somehow, she managed to create all kinds of scenarios where Greg ended up hurting her, but she had not shared that with anyone, especially Theory. Shaking away the invasive thoughts, Virtuous shifted her thinking to her art project.

Entering Sandy's office, Virtuous was on guard. Her body did not really want another fight, but she'd defend herself to the end. Greg was never controlling her again.

Cautiously, Virtuous glanced around. She did a 360-degree turn but saw nothing out of order; still, her guard was up. Something felt off about this interaction. It could be that she was being extremely paranoid, but her intuition was almost never wrong.

"Virtue, whatever are you doing?" Sandy asked accusingly, wearing her trademark Russian Red lipstick. Her hair was insanely neat and curled to perfection. Why a refined woman, who seemed to have good taste, be interested in pursuing Greg was beyond her.

Hearing the nickname *Virtue* caused Virtuous to pause. She hated that name and what it represented. It had been Greg's endearment for her, and hearing it now felt like an arrow through her heart. It brought back unwanted memories that she did her best to bury. That was why fear was ruling her heart. Her mind began to rehash the past.

Shaking off the chill and calming her anger, Virtuous glared at Sandy. "My name is Virtuous. Call me anything else, and I won't respond."

A shocked expression marred her nearly perfect alabaster face. "Excuse me. I didn't mean to upset you. I came to get you because you have a phone call. I'll step out so that you can have some privacy."

Before Virtuous could ask who was on the line, Sandy was gone. Shrugging her shoulder, Virtuous sat down in the plush leather office chair and picked up the phone, pressing the line that flashed a waiting call.

"Hello, this is Virtuous."

"Virtue."

Not him. "Greg?" Instantly her heartbeat increased, sweat beads formed on her forehead, and her breathing grew shallow. *Hang up!* her inner voice shouted, yet her body would not move. It was as if Greg's voice had paralyzed her. Every verse about facing her fears started to crumble. This man was not supposed to have power over her anymore.

"Of course, it's me. Anyway, darling, I just wanted to say I forgive you. I know you only attacked me because you thought I would hurt the girls, which I would never do. I get it. I know I upset you, but you know that was your fault for lying to me. Had you been honest, we could have avoided the entire incident."

Virtuous frowned, embittered and offended by his narcissism and complete dismissal of how it was his entire fault. Greg was a master at assigning blame and rewriting history to his benefit.

"Now, I need you to recant. You have my family upset and questioning my character. We can't have that. Not to worry, though, we can still fix this. I know about you going to the police and telling them lies. All you need to do is tell the truth. The truth is that Tommy made you lie. Okay? We know that Addison and Tommy are behind this to get custody of the girls."

There was a pause as if Greg was waiting for her to respond, and honestly, she was still attempting to process all he was saying.

"Listen to me; I miss you and I miss Tory. I want us all together again, and only you can make that happen, Virtue."

That was enough to pull her out of her momentary paralysis. Greg was no longer in charge, and she refused to give him any more power. "Never! I'm not a liar. You know what you did."

"Virtue, you're making a huge mistake. You either do as you're told, or your friends will suffer the consequences, and then you'll still end up right back with me. Let me be clear; I own you. You're mine. If you continue to refuse me, bad things might happen. That thug that has a juvie record, I'll make sure he's arrested again. Your so-called father that's locked up, it would be a shame for him to get hurt or even die. Riots happen all the time in prison. I can do that Virtue. I'm the police and can do whatever I want. Be a good girl and recant," he fumed. Gone was that endearing fatherly tone now replaced by a furious madman.

Normally, it would not have gotten this far, Virtuous would have easily given in to his demands and given him whatever he wanted, but no more. He had told that lie for the last time; being a police officer did not make him untouchable.

Hearing enough, Virtuous quickly hung up the phone. She took a second to compose herself before confronting Sandy. That woman had some nerve. She was a guidance counselor, a mandated reporter of suspected or known child abuse, yet she was helping Greg victimize her. *Not today Satan!*

The confrontation did not take long because as soon as Virtuous gathered her belongings, Sandy was re-entering the room. There was a knowing smirk on her face and harsh glare in her eyes as if Virtuous was intimidated by her. This woman was really feeling herself because of Greg.

"Really? You just pulled me in here to speak with Greg. What was the point of that?"

Sandy's dark eyes glared at her. "To talk some sense into you. Your father is a good man. While he was in Utah recovering, your mother's father went up there and threatened him. He vowed he would tell everyone that Greg was physically and sexually assaulting you. We both know that isn't true. He doesn't need you because he has me. You're just jealous of me being in your father's life. You simply want him for yourself, but he loves me. I'll be the new Mrs. Hartford, and when I am, you're not welcome to come back unless you recant your lies," Sandy accused.

At that moment, Virtuous could visualize herself slapping some sense into Sandy. However, that was not a plausible reaction. Instead, Virtuous had to do a triple-take.

Was this woman serious? Who wanted Greg's forty-year-old, mentally unstable, pedophile self? *Ew!* Women like Addison and Sandy really bothered her. They defended men like Greg, knowing they were monsters because they were too weak, or too desperate, to be alone. However, she was not confounded. This was how she imagined it would happen. Greg would still lose and so would Sandy. The level of pathetic she now displayed made Virtuous feel nothing but pity for her. Sandy had no idea what she was unleashing.

"Greg isn't my father. Fathers don't hurt their children. To be technical, since I was never adopted, he's my uncle. Note that what you just did was unprofessional and unethical, but what you won't do is re-victimize me. I know what Greg did; he knows what he did, and if you were smart, you'd see he's using you. I knew that was his plan all along. You fell right into his trap. I feel sorry for you, Sandy, so pathetic because Greg doesn't love you nor does he want you. He's using you to get to me. Be sure to stay away from me, or you'll hear from my attorney—and the authorities. Goodbye."

CHAPTER 17

Ezekiel sighed deeply. His large form was splayed across his assigned bunk bed as thoughts of the past and present ran through his mind like a movie. The game of *what-ifs* rested heavily on his heart. So many mistakes he made, so much deception he ever saw, not until now. It was ripping him apart.

Sleepless nights had become his new normal. There was too much on his mind; his children, all four of them, and the betrayal of a woman who said she loved him. The fact that his one, true love had been taken from him because of jealousy was like losing Valerie all over again. He had become the man her father said he was. His love for her was what got her killed. That was killing him. He thought Penelope was his saving grace, his second chance at getting it all right.

The woman he thought he knew stole six years of Theory's life. Her actions kept him from his son just so she could be with Ezekiel. The level of planning, lies, and manipulations it took to pull that off and keep it secret for years was disconcerting. It blew his mind and antagonized him all at once. Countless, innocent lives ruined over the bondage of jealousy, insecurity, lies, and loneliness.

The old Ezekiel would have sought revenge upon his release, but Theory sent him something, a Bible Study called KILL BILL, *Kneeling in the Lord's Love to defeat Bondage, Insecurity, Lies, and Loneliness.* That was what he had to do because if not, he would be sent back to prison, one far worse than he was currently occupying, and he would be separated from all his children again.

That was not an option. Something had to be done. Without a doubt, Ezekiel could not stay married to a murderer, especially a woman who killed his soulmate and true love. And for the first time in years, he wept.

A & Ω

Penelope had gotten her hair and nails done as she wanted to look her best for Ezekiel. She could not wait to see him and get an update about his other children. Hopefully, they would not want anything to do with him. The last thing she needed was for them to remind Big EZ of Valerie. Even in death, the heffa was a problem. Besides, her children should come first; they mattered the most, not his other children.

After some last-minute primping, she headed into the facility to see her man. After going through the process, she quickly prepared herself for Ezekiel. When she saw him, he did not look like his usual jovial self; something was terribly wrong. Penelope hoped he was not going to that dark place again. She knew his other children would bring him down.

"Hey, baby."

He nodded but remained mute. That was unlike him. Feeling the sting of how unaffected he was by her presence, she frowned before asking, "What's wrong, baby?"

Penelope observed his body language. The little vein in his forehead was on full display. He was displeased and upset about something, but she had no idea what. There was a detached coldness in his eyes, something she hadn't seen since he went dark after Valerie's death. Calming herself, she played her part of the clueless, loving wife. Leaning back, then moving forward, she propped her head on her fisted hand and stared lovingly at her husband.

"Penelope, you remember when you came in here and we talked about Nocturnal and Staci's situation? I told you that you better not be keeping secrets from me, and you were like, ' *What secret do I have?*"

Guilt assailed her as a lukewarm feeling overcame Penelope. Closing her eyes, she did her best to show no emotion. He knew something, and he was pissed. What did he know? She'd told so many lies that she had no idea which one was about to catch up with her.

Exhaling slowly, she opened her eyes and stared into her husband's eyes then she instantly knew. The answer she was searching for five minutes ago was in his eyes. She knew that he knew and that meant that Staci told on her. That disloyal, snitching heffa found God and sold her out. That was okay because once Penelope fixed this, she was going to pay Miss Staci a visit. "I…"

"Don't fix your lips to lie. I know the truth, I knew it the moment you sat down. I have no idea how I missed it before, but I see it so clearly now. You're evil, Penelope. Your lack of remorse, the constant cunning, and lies; you played me like a symphony. I thought you really loved and cared about me, but you only care about yourself."

Tears formed at the rims of her eyes. She could make him change his mind. She knew it. Penelope opened her mouth to speak, but he hushed her.

"This is what you're going to do. Wentworth's associate who does family law is going to bring you divorce papers, and you're going to sign them and contest nothing. You'll give sole custody of our children to me. In my stead, my mama will take them. Then you need to apologize to all my kids, the oldest for taking their mother away from them, and then the youngest for taking their mother away from them because you'll do time for your crimes. There's no statute of limitations on murder. You also need to apologize to Theory and his family. What you did to that boy, what I wanted to do to that boy because I thought he had hurt Valerie was wrong on every level."

"I love you, Ezekiel. I didn't mean to hurt nobody. I warned her," Penelope wailed.

Ezekiel shook his head. He finally saw Penelope for who she was, and it devastated his heart. "Ain't no man worth that Penelope. No man or woman is worth your freedom or your soul, and you forfeited both. And now, you have nothing. Be easy because Big EZ is done with you!" Then he nodded at the CO to take him back, and all Penelope could do was cry. She hated Valerie. How was she losing to a dead woman?

CHAPTER 18

Life had been hectic, and it seemed as if everything was happening at once, but then again when was that not happening? That was life, unpredictable and constantly changing.

That was just how Virtuous felt when she opened her email and had over one hundred emails from Greg although she could not prove it was it was him. But she knew it was him since he could not contact her through the school after what happened with Sandy.

For her safety, it was decided that she would attend school online. After the first of the year, they would reassess her status. With that knowledge, Greg was now cyber-stalking her. He was spoofing calls, sending obscene photos, and veiled threats, but what could she do when he was meticulously covering his tracks? He was breaking the law, but she could not prove it.

Greg's actions were slowly breaking her down. Prior to Greg finding out about Theory, he was more in control. There were times he lost it, but she was able to rein him back in. But not now. Greg was out of control and even more treacherous. Virtuous was nervous each time she left her apartment. Life was different now because she could not predict his moves or manage his moods. That left *what ifs* lingering in her mind.

Doing her best to steady her mind, she painted almost daily for her senior project, and other times, just to get out her emotions. They were all over the place. There was peace in prayer, but she could not quiet her mind enough to gather her thoughts.

Often, that kept her awake at night, so painting soothed her. Right now, she felt like David, as she, too, was running for her life. She was seeking God's assistance to stop her enemies. Greg and guilt were nipping at her sanity.

In those moments, she remembered the word*: Let not your heart be troubled, neither let it be afraid.* The battle between fear and faith, Greg and God, were at an all-time high. Ultimately, God would win, but at what cost to her? How many more bruises, internal and external, would she have to suffer?

There was a constant tug-of-war in her mind and heart. Telling the truth ruined a family, but keeping the lie was ruining her and dismantling her faith. Was she selfish to save herself? Didn't she have the right to defend herself? Didn't she have a right to live life unafraid?

"God help me. I'm struggling. I know what John 14:27 says, but right now, that verse isn't working. Sometimes, it feels like I'll survive this, and then other times, I feel like it's defeating me. I don't want to be the kind of Christian who loves You and praises You only during the good times. I want to love, trust, praise and obey You even when things are murky. Lord, these are dark times, and I'm scared.

"I fear more for my daughter, my new family, my Dad, and for Theory than I do myself. The ugliest of sins have been committed against me, and I'm still here. However, if anything happened to those, I love the most, I don't think I'll survive. Knowing Greg, he will do whatever horrid act to get what he wants.

"I know what jealousy and obsession can do; it made a woman murder my biological mother; it made my aunt attack me and allow me to be abused by her husband, and it has driven Greg insane. He has nothing now, and a man who has nothing to lose is willing to do anything. I don't know what to do or how to be proactive with a man who is unpredictable. I know when King David was sought after, when he was on the run for his life, You were there. Guide me, Lord. Give me Your peace, calm my heart and my mind. God, please don't let Greg take any more from me. What little I have left, whatever is left of my stolen virtue, I give to You. I'm not whole and probably never will be, but I give you what is left of me; just protect those I love. Don't let fear overtake me. Lastly, Father, may my offering, though scarred and shattered, be worthy of just a piece of Your peace and protection. For it's all I have Lord; it's all I have. In Jesus' name, Amen," she whispered.

"You're worthy, Proverbs, more than you'll ever know," the rich baritone uttered, causing a series of emotions to surge throughout Virtuous' body.

Just like that, warmth embraced her, and she turned and grinned at Theory. That man was created for her. There was nothing about

Theory that she did not love. Seeing him, hearing his voice was like instant manna to her heart.

In his eyes, she did feel worthy. Theory was her antidote. He took an unworthy girl and helped rebuild her; he loved her, knowing she was not whole. He promised to protect her when on one else would. Wiping her watering eyes, she whispered her gratitude to God for allowing her to love and be loved by a man like Theory.

His thick arms held her greatest treasure. Tory's small body was fully protected by Theory; that same loving expression was on his face. Theory adored Tory, and she adored him. There was one person missing from the party. Chauncory was his father's shadow. Since he was not wrapped around his daddy's leg then he must have fallen asleep on the ride over. "Did you get off work early?"

"Nope. The same time as always, but, um, are those my t-shirts folded up? You trying to tell me something?" he asked, amused.

"Oh, they don't smell like you anymore. I need you to fix that." She winked.

"Done. What's up? You're smiling and winking at me, but I feel like you're doing that to hide something. I know I walked in on you praying, and I wasn't trying to eavesdrop, but I know something is up. Talk to me, Proverbs," he probed, concerned, walking deeper in the room that she had set up as an art studio. Normally, she did not allow her daughter or Chauncory in the area because of the strong fumes, but today, she had only been sketching. It was her interpretation of David in the Book of Psalms on the run from his enemies. Instead of David, it was her running from Greg.

"No, I was just having a moment," she explained, trying to wave off the moment. "Serena said that would happen. You know, because I've buried a lot and it's all coming back. Sometimes, I get triggered and just get sucked back in that time and place, and I feel it all. It can be overpowering."

Theory shook his head understandingly, another trait she adored about him. Theory did not get mad or annoyed at her about her feelings. He just let her feel. He was her safe space.

"I'm sorry, Proverbs, but remember this; God is not of the past or will be in the future. He is a present, right now, on-time God. I hate that the past is coming back, but don't get lost where God isn't. Stay present, Proverbs. His name is I AM, not I was or I will be. Don't let the past imprison you. We all love you, and we all support you."

"I know. I just…man, what if what happened to Valerie happens to me?"

"Uh, baby, Staci's my only, ex and she knows better than to even speak your name. I promise you she's not that dumb. Everybody in the southeast knows I don't play about my Proverbs. Didn't I just tell you that God is not of the future but the present? Why are you creating problems where they aren't? We don't do *what-if*s; we do *what is*."

"I hear you, Theory, but I mean Sandy. Tamari said they're going to fire her, and I'm sure she'll blame me. I don't get it. Why is she willing to lose everything she has for a man who is only using her?"

Theory blew out a hard breath, kissed the top of Tory's head to soothe her, and then turned his attention back to Virtuous. "I think it comes back to the KILL BILL sermon. Take Staci for example; she claims the reason she lied to Nocturnal about Chauncory being his son was because I got locked up and she didn't want her child to grow up fatherless. Mind you, I was just in juvie, so she knew I was eventually getting out. They would have let me see my son, so I know that's a lie.

"She was cheating on me because she never had a father figure, you know. There was no man in her life to show her affection and teach her how a man should treat a woman and that caused insecurity. Staci was getting attention from men, so she fed on it. That was her downfall. Being with more than one guy made her feel special, I guess.

"Then with Penelope, she was and is still obsessed with Big EZ. It's not that she loves him it's that she wants to possess him. Back then, I was too young to peep game, but I can see it now. That kind of illogical thinking is dangerous and unnatural, but her father left after she was born. She has that mindset that nobody can leave her; she has this fear of loneliness. She's clingy and needy. I'm surprised she was able to function after Big EZ got arrested.

"Now, Sandy is a little of everything. Seems to me that she wants love and a man so badly that she'll overlook flaws. Greg knows just how to exploit her. Women like that are unstable because they'll do anything to get the outcome they seek. Baby, God isn't about to allow what happened to your mom, *may Valerie rest in peace*, happen to you."

Virtuous nodded her head and nibbled nervously on her bottom lip before replying, "You're right and well said. I see someone is doing the KILL BILL Bible Study."

"It's a lifesaver and really had me looking deeper into myself. We're parents, so we got to do better, right? Chauncory and Tory are watching every move we make. When I act now, I do so with the understanding that these kids will move like I move, and for them, I have to be right."

"Okay, I see you with that Solomon wisdom. You're right." Virtuous paused for a moment and thanked God for Theory, again. This man was forever amazing her. Never in her life did she even dream a man like this existed. That was Theory, always trying to be better, and he loved so thoroughly and authentically that she often wondered what a man like that wanted with her.

"So, are you and Stanley talking now?" It was a situation that she did not get in the middle of. She knew that when Theory was ready, he would talk to his father, and she did not push it.

"I've spoken to him, but we'll probably never have the relationship he wants. Besides, I think he has a lady friend. Anyway, I don't know that I'll ever fully trust him like a son trusts a father," Theory confessed. Then he went quiet, and Virtuous could tell he was thinking about something. She was about to ask when he spoke up first.

"Come on, let's take the kids out and get something to eat. I'm famished."

Virtuous giggled; he was so extra. She was sure he raided the kitchen before coming to see her. "Can we go to Manny's?"

"Wherever you want to go is good with me. Oh, I'm staying over tonight. I got one of those blowup beds for me and Chauncory to sleep on. We'll post up in the family room. Cool?"

"That's great," she agreed as she got up from the chair. Theory waited for her and she reached in for a hug and a kiss. A warm sensation flowed through her body. Yep, he was her antidote.

"I love you, Virtuous. We're going to get through this; like the song says, '*I've learned to worship You…my circumstance doesn't even stand a chance*'," he sang in his velvety baritone.

"Okay, William Murphy, because *praise is what I do*! I love you."

A & Ω

As Theory drove to the restaurant, he occasionally glanced at Virtuous. There was a smile on her face but agony in her eyes. Most people would not notice it because she was an expert at hiding her feelings. She had to in order to survive years of abuse, but she could not hide from him. He was her heart, after all, so he knew when her emotions were off.

Serena told him and his family since they were Virtuous's main source of support that this would be a tough time for her. Serena also warned them about secondary trauma and offered to provide family therapy as well. Theory knew that Virtuous required extra care and thoughtfulness.

Recently, Theory got a glimpse of just how much she was struggling with telling the truth because doing so hurt others. Virtuous, no matter what was done to her, did not like to hurt anyone. He saw how her heart was breaking by looking at her drawings and paintings. A part of her felt empathy for the Hartford family. She and Theory were extremely different on that level.

There was no sorrow or sympathy in his heart for the Hartford family or Sandy. Whether they knew or not of the abuse itself, they should have known something was wrong. Addison was just as guilty, if not more, as Greg was. What kind of aunt/mother would allow something so disgusting to continue? That was the part he could not get over yet. Eventually, he would get there but not now. Theory did not want Tory to interact with any of them except Jason and Maddison. Right or wrong, that was how he felt. It was his job to protect the ones he loved, and he loved Proverbs and Tory.

Reaching over Theory gently placed his hand on top of Virtuous' soft one. He noticed after the attack that she was jumpier, and he did his best to make his presence known when he was around so that he would not startle her. He was careful about the way he held or touched her, not wanting to trigger any more traumatic memories. He took his cues from her, not making any assumptions.

He felt her squeeze his hand, causing him to look at her once they made it to a red light.

"Something wrong?"

"No. I'm just thankful. Some girls in my situation don't have a supportive team like I do. I know it's going to be a tough road ahead, but I have so many people who believe me and love me." Then she shook her head. "Don't mind me; I'm all over the place emotionally. My moods and my mental state change every minute. I try to be grateful, no, I *am* grateful. It could always be worse. I'm here and I'm alive, and I need to be thankful for that."

For a moment, Theory just allowed the moment to be. He was in awe of her maturity and wisdom. If he suffered the way she did at her age, he would not be able to react like her.

"I'm thankful for you. I was thinking instead of staying here for Thanksgiving that we plan a trip to Six Flags Over Georgia and the Georgia Aquarium; you love stuff like that."

"Really?" Her eyes lit up like lightning bugs on a dark, country night. Sometimes, he forgot just how young she was. Right now, he could see how much of her childhood was stolen from her.

"Yeah, why not? We can take the kids. I know Valor would love it, as would Shalamar and Archie. You know they're just big ole kids. We need to do something special like that. Remember, we're making good memories.

"That would be great. I've never had that kind of fun. A real vacation," she hummed.

Theory was in shock by her reaction. Even he had gone on family vacations before he was locked up. "You've never been on a vacation?"

"Not fun ones; a vacation was just another way for Greg to have his way with me. I hated them, but I want to go with you. I've never been to Six Flags."

Rage surged through Theory. Greg really ruined everything. He intentionally forbade her to have good and happy memories, all in an effort to completely control her. This man really wanted to own her, body, mind, and soul. It irritated him. If only he could confront Greg. However, Theory knew for a fact that Greg would never step to him because he was a dirty, debauched dastard.

"I promise that I'll always make it my mission to provide you with the best memories. No more talking about what used to be; let's talk about what is and what can be," he soothed as he pulled into Manny's.

After parking, they collected the children and headed inside, feeling as if there were eyes on them, Theory looked around but saw no one. He felt Virtuous tense beside him. "It's cool, Proverbs."

She nodded, but Theory could tell that she was a little nervous and that bothered him. His girl was not about to live in fear every time she went somewhere because Greg thought that being a cop made him above the law.

A & Ω

Once the food arrived, the all-around mood changed. Chauncory was sitting beside Virtuous, resting his head on her arm, and Tory was glued to Theory with her head nestled in his neck, only letting go when she saw the steaming plate of pasta. Baby girl liked to eat. The only person missing was Cutie.

"Can I say the blessing, Daddy?" Chauncory asked.

"Yes."

Just as Chauncory finished the prayer, a car alarm went off. Theory instantly got up to see if it were Proverbs' SUV because, for some reason, he really felt like someone was watching them. When he walked outside, he saw that the SUV had been vandalized, and there was a sticky note hanging on the shattered windshield.

Cautioning Proverbs to stay back with the children, Theory picked up the note that simply read, *End It!*

Greg made his move. A cowardly move, but a move, nonetheless. However, he still was not man enough to confront Theory. Theory was aching for a confrontation. Their time was coming...

CHAPTER 19

It was midmorning as Staci entered the hospital with Sadie to visit Nocturnal. She wanted to show Nocturnal pictures of Selma who was slowly improving and hopefully would be home, hopefully for Christmas or by the New Year. There was concern over Selma having an intellectual disability, but Staci was simply grateful that her baby was alive and that was the best blessing.

"Mama, you think Daddy will like the teddy bear?" Sadie asked, bringing Staci out of her thoughts. Sadie's round brown eyes glowed with excitement. This little girl loved her daddy.

"Of course. That's a get-well Vermont Teddy Bear. He'll adore it just like Selma adores hers. You and Chauncory did a good job picking those out," Staci cooed as they arrived at Nocturnal's room.

Sadie let go of Staci's hand and burst inside. "Daddy, I got you a surprise! This is for you, so you can get better like Selma," Sadie rushed, her little voice bouncing throughout the room. Staci noticed how Sadie just climbed on the bed, not caring that a nurse was trying to check his vitals or that one of her father's legs was missing. Nope, she only had eyes for her daddy, and his imperfections went unnoticed. That made Staci smile.

"Runt 2, you got that for me?" he asked as the nurse exited the room, allowing them their privacy.

"Yes, me and Chauncey, but he's not here. He's with his other daddy, Mr. Theo. He's nice. He bought me this outfit."

Staci almost said something, but Nocturnal waved her off. "Me and Mr. Theo are cool. We quashed the past and decided to move forward as men and fathers, so calm your shaky nerves. For real, thank you for bringing my baby to see me."

That took Staci by surprise. Maybe having her pastor come see Nocturnal was changing him?

"How's it going?" Staci asked.

Nocturnal lifted a curious brow. "You want to know the truth?"

"Of course, I do."

"I'm doing. I'm depressed some days, angry other days, and I miss my best friend. I'm lonely. My mom hasn't been down here in a while, but I know the traveling is hard on her. I ain't even talking to Penelope after her foul moves. I keep holding on because of Chauncey, Sadie, and Selma. That's all I got, for real. Not one of my goons has come to see about me, just you, Theory, and Lourdes. Now, I know who got me."

Staci dropped her head. "They'll come around. They're still grieving Congo."

"And I'm not? I got to deal with his death and know that I caused it! All I do in this bed is grieve. I grieve for my best friend and his family. I grieve for myself because I look like an alien. Half of my dreads are gone. I got staples in my head, and I can't even bathe myself properly without assistance. I'm pissing in a bag and laying on a bedpan. I don't even feel real.

"They're talking about a prosthetic leg like I'm a robot. I'm not 'Nocturnal' anymore. I don't know who I am. I blame you for that Staci. You know what my children mean to me. You could have dealt with it better than you did. Now, I'll be separated from them because you know being a black man, they're going to make an example out of me. I won't be there to see my daughters grow up. I'm grieving that, too. How about you just leave and let me and Sadie spend some time together?"

That escalated quickly. Staci was aghast by the request. She knew he was hurt by her lie, but she had hoped that he would forgive her by now. The fact that he still blamed her aggrieved her soul. "I'm sorry about what I did. If I could undo it, I would. I pray one day you'll forgive me."

"You got some nerve." Penelope's iced voice penetrated the room. The entire room instantly became chilled. It was as if Penelope was Emma Frost.

Staci turned and watched as Penelope sashayed into the room. She looked pissed. "I don't want any problems, Penelope. Chill because you see Sadie's in here."

"Then you shouldn't have run your mouth off to my husband. Just because you ain't got a man don't mean you go messing with another person's relationship. With your 'Bible-toting, I'm better than everyone else attitude'. You're no saint; you still an *ain't.*"

"I didn't tell Big EZ nothing!" Staci defended. She was annoyed that Penelope would even assume that.

"I did," Nocturnal answered smoothly. "I told him after Theory came down here to see me. Theory thought I helped set him up because I wanted Staci, but I had no idea what you were doing. That was wrong, P. Your one deceptive action was a domino effect; you messed up bad. Don't come down here bothering Staci. You kept her lie from me; she kept your lie for as long as she could. Y'all even. Now, both of y'all gotta deal with the consequences of your actions. Oh, and both of y'all get out of my room. I'm trying to spend quality time with my daughter."

With that, Staci shook her head but collected her stuff to leave. She handed the pictures of Selma over to Nocturnal and made her way out of the room.

Staci made it a good two feet before her neck jerked back, and Penelope started to attack her. Staci didn't fight back; she just blocked hits. "Stop Penelope!" Staci always knew Penelope was short a few cups of sugar, but this was just insane.

"Mama!" Sadie screamed, terrified at witnessing her mother's assault.

"Yo, I'm calling the nurse to call security if y'all don't quit. Act like adults. Y'all see my baby in here!" Nocturnal fumed, pulling Sadie into him, telling her to close her eyes and cover her ears.

Staci just fell to the floor and curled into a ball. When the blows stop coming, she unfolded herself to see that security had Penelope against the wall and she was just cussing and fussing, looking every bit the crazed fool that she was.

A & Ω

"Hey, Theo, I see you got the kids with you," Deacon Hayes greeted bending down to shake Chauncory's hand before tickling Tory's cheek. She offered him a smile before burying herself back into Theory.

"Yeah, Virtuous and Valor are dealing with some legal stuff. I told her I'd bring Tory with me."

"That's great; you want to let them play while we talk?"

"Yeah, Chauncory has his kid Kindle Fire, but this one here; she's attached to my hip. Has been ever since the night that Proverbs got attacked. If I put her down, she starts whining and lifting her hands. If you don't mind, I'll just hold her."

"I understand. Is that what you want to talk about today? When I was praying this morning, God laid the passage of Romans 12:17-21 and Matthew 5:43-48 on my heart."

Theory immediately recognized the verses. Romans 12 was about not repaying your enemies with vengeance because vengeance is the Lord's, and Matthew 5 was about loving your enemies, and yeah, that's exactly what he needed to hear. Couldn't God just let him have a moment to track Greg down, beat him mercilessly, and then let him remember to love his enemy and let God have vengeance?

Letting out a guilty sigh, all Theory could do was nod his head. "Deacon Hayes, man, this is getting out of hand. Dude busted the windshield, while my family and I were out to eat. Thank God, for Safelite. Then he put a sticky note on her SUV saying *End it* like I'm just going to run scared. I was so livid. He put my family at risk. I can't get that look of fear Virtuous had out of my mind.

"She's terrified, and I know she is because he's stalking her, calling her, and using other people to threaten her, but she can't prove it because he knows the law. She doesn't even sleep through the night, not even when I stay over. I'm pissed. I wanted to hurt him, for real. I know that's not aligned with Christianity, but this dude needs to be stopped. He's stolen her virtue; he's stolen her freedom; he's stealing her joy, and I can't let him take any more from her. What kind of man would I be to just do nothing? I want to marry Proverbs. I know for a fact that she is the one God made just for me, Tory might not be mine biologically, but she's my child, the same as Chauncory. My kids won't live like this. I trust God, I do, but I would appreciate if He moved more swiftly in this situation. I don't know how much more Proverbs can take. I won't let her suffer; I won't."

Deacon Hayes sat back and listened, his eyes never leaving Theory's. "Theory, you amaze me. To be such a young man, you really have your mind in the right place, I tell you. I hate what Virtuous has suffered and how it's impacted you both. Here is what I'm suggesting you do. Read five Psalms and one chapter of Proverbs daily for thirty days; do it with Virtuous, too. Also, do a Daniel fast and make sure you both journal, or, in her case, paint. Then I want you to just be in God, in silence for ten uninterrupted minutes; do nothing but be still and know that God is present. When you feel the urge to seek revenge, when your heart is beating to the battle of war and violence, pray. You put on your whole armor of God and you don't allow the Devil that has snared your enemy to ensnare you.

"Like you said, you have a family and you want to marry Virtuous. Well, you can't be the husband she needs if your first thought is to be reactionary. You need to react like the Word teaches us. If you don't, Virtuous will surely suffer, and you don't want that. Do you understand me?

"I know that seems backward, but you need to remember that God is already victorious, that He is a God that protects His children. He is still working, even when it feels like He's moving moderately. Psalm 27:14 tells us to *wait on the Lord.*" Deacon Hayes paused to let what he said sink in before continuing.

"I saw this post one day, and the person asked, *God why are you sending me through this storm?* It was a picture of massive waves and lightning. I tell you it was a furious storm, and God answered *because your enemies can't swim.* Greg can't swim. He's drowning in sin. However, you and Virtuous can, and not only that, but God is your lifejacket. Yes, to you God may be moving casually, but He is an on-time God, never late, never early, but on time. He is faithful to His children. You, son, are His child, just like Tory, Chauncory, and Virtuous; y'all are covered. Greg is already defeated. Your weapons are prayer and faith, not payback or fear. You're a descendant of the King of Kings. The power that He has is in you. Can't nobody defeat the One who overcame death. That's the God you serve. That's the God who protects you. Don't let this situation cause you to sin; let this situation show you that God always wins."

Theory teared up after that. Deacon Hayes always got him like that, made him rethink his anger, and redirect his energy. He was right. If he allowed himself to stoop to Greg's level, he would leave behind his son, Tory, and Virtuous, and they all needed him. He needed to be faithful and patient at this moment and let God do what He does. Theory could only see what was in front of him, but God saw all. "I hear you, and I agree."

"Let's pray."

"Can I pray, too?" Chauncory asked, putting his Kindle down. Theory could not help but smile. His son was something special.

"You sure can," Deacon Hayes agreed as they formed a circle and bowed their hands.

Once the prayer was over, Theory thanked Deacon Hayes again.

"No thanks needed. I want to see you win. I want to be at your and Virtuous' wedding. Y'all are good kids that got handed a bad deck. I've never seen either of you use your pasts as excuses not to improve and better yourselves. The resilience you both have is commendable. You're practically babies raising babies, and you're doing a fine job. God is using both of you to do amazing things. Don't ever doubt that. Don't ever doubt how important you are to the Father."

"Yes, sir," Theory replied as he gathered the children. "Oh, I won't be here next week. I'm taking the kids and Proverbs, along with a few of our friends, down to Atlanta to celebrate Thanksgiving. We all need a change of scenery."

"I respect that. We can still talk. Just call me, and we'll do our session over the phone or Skype."

Theory chuckled. "I can do that."

"Theo, it's going to be okay. I'm always here."

"I know. I appreciate and love you for it. What you said today, I needed to hear that. I'm here for you, too. I know you're my mentor, but I also pray for you. You remind me a lot of Pop, and I know if he were alive, he'd like you, too. Thanks for looking beyond my past and seeing what I could be and not what I was."

"Boy, get on out of here before you have me crying. One day, you'll be the mentor; you'll be the one ministering to another in need," he teased as he embraced Theory.

Theory laughed and so did Chauncory, not that he had any clue what he was laughing for. "We out."

"Peace," Chauncory added before grabbing his daddy's hand.

Deacon Hayes and Theory both laughed.

CHAPTER 20

Nocturnal was being pushed into his room by his physical therapist, Quinton. Thanks to adopting a better attitude, Nocturnal was able to dominate the rigorous workout. It felt better to do something proactive than to be lying in bed, reliving the past and feeling sorry for himself. Besides, Quinton was a street dude like him and took no attitude. Dude almost made Nocturnal want to box him until he remembered he was one leg down. Now, they were cool.

This was why they were joking with each other, and Nocturnal was caught up, laughing and not paying attention to his surroundings. He had not noticed that his normally shut door was open. Once they entered his room, his eyes were fully opened, and they connected with someone he had not seen in weeks, a person he thought he would never see again. His heart nearly stopped.

There stood Willamina Kabila, Congo's mother, wearing her signature *dhuku*. Her dark brown eyes still held sadness, the kind of grief one would expect from a mother who had buried a son and already lost a husband. At that moment, the entire accident went through Nocturnal's mind, and he could not look away from Mama Kabila. No, because he knew he was the cause of her agony, and nothing he did, no apology or guilt would ever heal her wounds. In some ways, she lost two sons. He knew he would never be welcomed into her life.

Whatever hardcore street that was in him melted away. He was at her mercy. It was from her whom he needed to hear forgiveness. It was she who controlled his fate, and if she berated and rejected him, he would never fix his mouth to disrespect her. She had every right to hate him and remove him from her life. Yet, every fiber in his body prayed she would offer him a second chance. She would give him the mercy he had not given others.

"Mama Kabila?" he mumbled. The softness of his voice was laced with boyish wanting.

A gentle smile brushed her face, and her grief-stricken eyes lit up for a moment.

"I'm sorry. I'm sorry I let my anger and jealousy take your son from you. If I could've died in his place, I would have. If I could redo it all, I would've acted differently. Congo was my best friend and my brother." He paused and dropped his head. The shame of his mistake was overwhelming. "I never meant for this to happen, Mama Kabila. I'm so sorry," he murmured as hard tears trailed down his face.

Those tears caused Mama Kabila to cry, and it was then that Nocturnal realized they were not alone. He knew Quinton was still in the room, but he had not seen that there was another person until the man pulled Mama Kabila into an embrace.

He was tall with light brown skin. His rustic eyes were glossy with unshed tears. He wore slacks and a button-down shirt with the sleeves rolled up. He had that suburban dad look perfected. However, there was something familiar about him. Nocturnal turned to him and nodded his head in greeting. "Um, you look like somebody I know," Nocturnal stated as he cleaned his face with the backside of his hand.

"You might remember me. I'm Stanley Campbell, Theory's father. I just came to be a support to Willamina. I know you two need to talk, so I can sit out in the waiting room and give you privacy."

Tilting his head slightly, Nocturnal looked at Mama Kabila for what she wanted to do. Obviously, Stanley meant something to her. She was completely comfortable in his embrace. As far as Nocturnal could remember, Willamina was only about her son after the death of his father. So, the appearance of a new man, Theory's father at that, was shocking. Still, he could see that there was something between them. "Mama Kabila, it's up to you."

"Stay," her soft voice hummed. Stanley nodded and then eased back to one of the chairs in the room, Quinton locked Nocturnal's wheelchair and exited the room, making sure to close the door behind him.

"I'm sorry, too, Percival. I know you've suffered greatly. At first, I blamed you, simply because I had so much anger in me. I was full of regret and hurt that I needed someone to lash out at. It was easy to curse your name. That was wrong. Since I've buried my son, I've been in deep prayer seeking guidance from God." She nodded then sniffled before continuing. Nocturnal was on the edge of his wheelchair, holding on to every word she said. He thirsted for her forgiveness and her love.

"I don't want to lose you, too. I forgive you. My heart and head know that you would never intentionally put Congo's life at risk. You were the one who took that bullet for him five years ago. You two always protected each other. I don't want you to do years in prison for a mistake. Lord knows the fact that you lost so much in one day is punishment enough. You've more than learned your lesson. I pray they won't charge you, and if they do that it's a light sentence. I'm prepared to help in any way that I can.

"You know, Norma Jean is pregnant; she's having a girl. She assured me that it would be best if I raised her and that she'll sign away her parental rights. I want Adama, that's what I've named her, to know her father's best friend. So, survive this, okay? I know it's hard and lonely. I've been more zombie-like than human, but knowing my son's daughter will be here soon is my motivation to keep pushing through. Don't give up and forgive me for taking so long to come and tell you this. Please know that I still love you."

As she finished talking, she walked up to Nocturnal and pulled him into a much-needed hug. He broke. He sobbed like a newborn baby. Everything hit him at once. He wrapped his arm around her waist and buried his head in her stomach. "I miss him. I don't know how I'ma make it. I promise you I won't give up. I'ma do my part as uncle to his daughter and son to you. Thank you for forgiving me. I don't deserve it."

"None of us do, but God forgave us, so we must forgive each other. Now, let go of any guilt or shame; be free, son; be free."

Nocturnal pulled back and just glared at her. "You sound like Staci's pastor. He keeps telling me to let go and come to God. I told him ain't no God for a goon. Ol' dude is persistent. You think if I confess to God, He can free me of all my sins? You know I'm no church boy."

"I know that He can, and He will. All you need to do is ask. God is bigger than any past, and His love surpasses all understanding. God loves you, Percival Kershaw. He knows you by name and the number of hairs on your head. You are His; all you have to do is accept and believe."

"I killed my best friend. I cheated on Staci, and I wanted to hurt an innocent man because of my own paranoia. And you're telling me God loves me? That He wants me in His family? I ain't worthy, Mama Kabila. All I know is the streets."

Willamina cupped his face. "You are worthy. Let me tell you about King David. He got a married woman pregnant after lusting over her. Then after failing to get her husband Uriah to go home, he had him placed on the frontlines of a battle, knowing the result would be death. He wanted to hide his sin. God still loved him and used him. King David felt God's wrath; however, God didn't let him go, He chastised him; still, He loved David. What I'm saying is God can use anyone. When Jesus died on the cross, He was not alone; there were two others there. They were guilty, but He was guiltless. In Luke, Chapter 23, the good thief, who knew Jesus had done no wrong and was the Son of God, had one request; he simply asked for Jesus to remember him when He came into His kingdom. You know what Jesus told him?"

Nocturnal had no clue but waited with bated breath for her to reveal the next part. Willamina smiled and continued, "Jesus said, 'Today, you will be with me in paradise'. So, you see, Jesus died on the cross for everyone. Even the thief. And that thief, for all his wrongs, knew who held his life. He'll do the same for you.

"We can all have eternal life with the One. My child, broken and sinful you may be, but we all are; we're still God's masterpieces."

Nocturnal was not sure if he believed he could have a relationship with God, but he wanted to do anything to make Mama Kabila smile again.

CHAPTER 21

The fresh December morning air wrapped around Virtuous' body, causing her to slightly shiver. The snickerdoodle-flavored hot cocoa warmed her hands as she gently blew on it before taking a sip. Her eyes danced across the populated ice-skating rink with joy.

Downtown Spartanburg had an outdoor ice rink that the children were eager to visit. Today, they finally got their wish.

After much thought, Virtuous decided to forgo her Winter Ball. Instead, she opted to spend the day with family and friends. Virtuous decided, instead, that attending prom would be the only event she participated in. By then, things with Greg would be settled and her bio-father would probably be released.

A smile ripped across Virtuous's face as she watched Tory wrap her little body around Theory's leg. He had been standing by, like a sentinel, since their arrival, his eyes fixed on Cordy, Chauncory, and Sadie.

Each child held the hand of an adult as they attempted to ice skate. Theory's friends, Shalamar and Archie, had volunteered to assist. Every day, she thanked God for Theory, his family, and his friends. They were so accepting and helping.

Virtuous was not an ice skater and chose to watch and record with her cell phone. It was moments like this that she was even more thankful for Theory. He promised her good memories, and so far, he was doing an outstanding job.

Now that she was going to therapy a few times a week, the fear and shame were lifting. Her relationship with God was stronger than ever. The way life was flowing now just made Virtuous peacefully content. She could not wait to spend Christmas with Theory and her paternal family.

The greatest blessing of discovering her father was meeting his family. Her father's side of the family was comical.

Recently, she and Valor met their siblings Evie, which was short for Evonne, and Evan. Evan took to Valor like they had known each other their entire lives. He was officially Valor's shadow. Evie was sweet but more standoffish. Both favored Ezekiel more than she and Valor. According to GG, her father's mother, Virtuous looked like her Aunt Erica. That was one person she had not met. Erica lived in Japan with her military husband, Jephte. They had spoken over the phone, and Virtuous could not wait to see her in person.

As if he sensed her looking at him, Theory lifted Tory in his arms and turned Virtuous. It was a perfect pose for the two, and she quickly snapped a picture. Tory's little cheeks were candy apple red from the cooler temperatures. A gentle breeze came, and Tory buried her head into Theory's neck, and he chuckled. It warmed Virtuous' heart how close the pair was. This was how a father was supposed to interact with a child. Not how Greg had treated her, but she was learning to let that pain go.

Seconds later, the pair was headed her way. They were all smiles, but Theory's demeanor quickly changed. For a moment, Virtuous was confounded. The intense glare in his eyes caused her concern. Then she heard, "Vivi."

Turning slightly, she saw the Hartford crew, minus Greg and LeAnn. Maddison shot by Cary and came charging toward Virtuous. It was a surprise to see her old family. She knew that Cary was coming and wanted to bring Maddison. Jason had told her that, but she had no idea about the others.

"Vivi, I missed you," Maddison's sweet, little voice hummed.

Virtuous closed her eyes as she inhaled her sister's scent. "I missed you too, sweetheart." Virtuous picked her up and twirled her around until they both were dizzy. She put her sister down, steadied her, and kissed the top of her head. "Go see Tory and Theory."

Maddison nodded and skipped the short distance to where Theory was waiting for her.

"Vivi." Papaw's voice was full of emotion, and his eyes were already watering. Just hearing him speak her name made her feel his agony. Most of her life, he had been the only other man in it. Unlike Greg, her grandfather had brought light in her life. Leaving him had been heartbreaking but necessary.

Virtuous smiled at him. He did not give her a moment to speak; he just pulled her into an embrace. "I'm sorry, sweetheart. Never would I have imagined my own son would do something so ungodly and ugly. Shame on me for not noticing. Please forgive me. I know you might hate me because I raised Greg, but I didn't raise my son to become a monster. I don't condone his actions."

"I know, Papaw. It's okay." Virtuous knew they would have a conversation at some point, but she had not thought it would be in a public setting. However, no one was close or even paying them any attention.

"No, it ain't," he huffed, the tears finally falling. "You didn't deserve none of what happened, and we should have done better by you. Now that I know the truth, I can see it all clearer. Annie wanted to come, but she's so torn up and ashamed of how she acted before. We believe you. Greg knows it. I want you to come back home, but I know you ain't comfortable anymore."

"I'm not. It wouldn't be a good idea anyway. I appreciate your apology, though you don't owe me one. You didn't know, and when you did, you reacted the way most people would. You've only seen the side of your son he wanted you to see, whereas I've seen all sides of him. If you need to hear it then I forgive you. Go see Tory because I'm sure she misses you."

He hugged her once more and then walked to where Theory was still standing, although not alone. Virtuous realized that Theory was joined by Valor and their friends. The children were taking a break, she assumed.

"We're sorry, too, Vivi," Cate and Norman chorused. "Your uncle knew before the rest of us. He said he felt something was off. When the truth came out, he wanted to come to you, but they wouldn't let us. I understand, I do. Please, don't think that we didn't believe you or that we didn't care.

Norman shook his head in agreement. "I'm sorry, Vivi. Don't think because you weren't born into the family that we don't love you. We do. I'm still your uncle, and you're still my niece. I'd take down any man that hurt you, even my brother. Whatever you need, whenever you need it, just ask. I owe you a lot. I should've picked up on it sooner, but as long as there is breath is in my body, I won't let him hurt you again," Norman vowed and pulled her into a warm embrace.

His declaration had her in tears. This, she did not expect. In fact, she thought they would all react like LeAnn had. "Don't cry, sweet girl. No more tears, no more of that. You're still everything God created you to be. Greg doesn't own you, and his sins against you are not your burdens to bear," he cooed, running his hand through her hair.

Virtuous nodded. She was so enwrapped in the conversation that she had not noticed anyone behind her.

"Who y'all?" Gina's rough voice interrupted. She had her hand on her wide hips, her dark eyes glaring daggers. "I'm GG, her paternal grandmama. I'on know y'all."

Cate looked up and offered a smile. "I'm Cate, her aunt. This is my husband Norman, her uncle, and that's our son Cary."

"Oh, you're the *others*. I know whatcha brother did to my baby. If you over here to try something, let me tell you, I ain't the one. I'm licensed to carry and carry I do. You upset my grandbaby, and I'll have half of Greenville and all of Anderson down here right and ready."

Virtuous wanted to laugh. GG was the best grandmama ever. Upon first meeting her, Virtuous was a little thrown by her unfiltered vernacular, but it took no time to warm up to her.

Gina "GG" All was not one to trifle with. Every word she spoke, she meant. Poor Cate was redder than a strawberry, and Norman just stared in awe. Cary slowly started edging backward as if he feared for his life. He should've because Granny could and would shoot. She loved God, guns, and cigarettes.

"We come in peace," Cate added.

Virtuous exploded into a fit of giggles that had her stomach cramping. Cate was so sincere. That did not stop GG from eyeing her harshly. She pursed her lips and finally nodded her acceptance. "C'mon, baby girl, let's get these babies something warm to drink."

A & Ω

Greg was incensed. His family was now refusing to allow him to visit Maddison. Since the DNA came back and proved that he was Tory's father and that Virtue was the mother, the situation had gone left. Never had he imagined a time when he would be unable to control Virtue. Now, he was on the outside looking in.

Right before his eyes, his own family was accepting Virtuous' new family. He blamed Addison; this all started because of her drug use and lies. Suddenly, she gets clean and wants to have a conscience. But look where she ended up. Locked in his basement. It was bad enough that Virtue had replaced him and let another man play daddy to their daughter, but for his own family accepting this madness was too much.

Now, he's the bad guy. The same people at his church who were backing him were now turning their backs because Virtue would not recant. The fact that Sandy got fired for helping him made her more annoying and needier than Addison ever was. He should have locked her up in the basement as well.

Greg thought he was so clever the way he was messaging Virtue. He had been doing it successfully for a while. Then someone used his tactics against him and placed a virus on his computer. He had to pull back because if he were found in violation of the court order, they would arrest him.

Now that Montez was also against him, many of his brothers in blue were turning their backs also. They all thought he was a pedophile.

Things were quickly getting out of hand, and he needed to get his daughters, and Virtue, and leave the country. Jason made his choice, as did his parents and brother. They were no longer his family, and he was done with them. He only needed his girls.

The only choice Virtue had was him. He would have her. If that little hoodlum she fancied herself in love with attempted to intervene, he was going down as well.

The little Winter Ball was happening soon, and he would move his plan into action. His mother still loved him. Greg was sure he could manipulate her into assisting him. Then he and the girls would be on their way.

Just as he was about to leave his vantage point, he saw a woman. She was walking with purpose, her eyes deranged. It looked as though she was speaking to herself. Negativity and evil rolled off her like smoke after an extinguished fire. Her right hand patted her pocket as if she were checking for something. His police training told him that she was carrying a concealed weapon.

Why was that necessary? It was midmorning; families were enjoying the rink, but this woman had no children. She carried no ice skates. Something was off about her.

Slowly getting out of his truck, he shadowed her. He'd wanted to stay out of sight, but something told him that he needed to keep an eye on this troubled woman, so he followed her. Her eyes turned from Virtuous to her brother Valor. It was then that she retrieved the hidden weapon in her pocket. She was about ten yards away, close enough to take them both out.

No one noticed her until she yelled, "You two were supposed to be dead! You'll die now!"

CHAPTER 22

Pandemonium and chaos reigned for what seemed like forever.

Echoes of gunshots, shouts, screams, and cries polluted the winter air. It took a moment to realize what was happening as pain seared through her leg. The mad ravings of her father's wife filled the air then more gunshots ensued. First, her thoughts were on the children then Theory and the rest of her family. *Where were they? Had death claimed those she loved?*

Paralyzed.

Virtuous' mind said go, but her body refused to listen. It was reminiscent of when Greg attacked her. Greg. In all this time, Virtuous thought if anything ever happened that the only danger, she would need to be concerned about was Greg, possibly Addison, but she was wrong.

She had apparently miscalculated just how angry her father's wife really was. Strange how Virtuous had never met the woman who had murdered her birth mother and manipulated her father. Now, Virtuous and Valor were her competition, her enemies whose presence needed to be eliminated.

This was madness.

Fight. Persevere. Survive. She mentally chanted as her body began to shut down. Her energy was low, and her body was burning from what she could only assume was a gunshot wound.

Was death coming? Can't die. She refused to leave her daughter motherless. *Whenever I am afraid, I will trust in You. In God (I will praise His word), in God I have put my trust; I will not fear. What can flesh do to me?* That verse from Psalms 56:3-4 was ingrained in her mind. She held on to it because it was her lifeline.

Theory probably had no clue how valuable that verse he texted would be. Every morning, he texted her a verse, and she texted him a prayer. It was their morning ritual. Would that be their last text?

That was the last thought she had before closing her eyes.

A & Ω

"You two were supposed to be dead! You'll die now!" The timbre was hard and full of rage. The entire rink appeared to still as that rage and hate polluted the area. Before Theory could turn to see who was speaking, he heard GG scream, "No, Penelope!"

Penelope? Theory mentally pondered and then it hit him. Theory knew exactly what Penelope intended on doing. She was the threat that he had not seen coming. His ignorance at underestimating her was about to cost him everything. Theory thought that Big EZ had his soon-to-be ex-wife under control—he thought wrong.

Penelope was near foaming at the mouth as she raved and cursed at her husband's older children. He was about to run towards her when another man got their first. The man was unknown to Theory until Maddison said 'Daddy'. He hadn't seen Greg since he first met Proverbs, but the man didn't look the same.

The emotions that shot through him were beyond description. Fear momentarily incapacitated his ability to move or think. Theory was in a haze. In slow motion, he heard the gunshots, the pounding of scared feet fleeing from the danger, and the screeching screams of the children—his sister, son, and daughter.

Theory leaped into action, securing the children nearest to him. He made himself a human shield, pulling them into his body. He glanced up and noticed that Virtuous was down. He felt a sinking feeling in his heart. That anxiety seized his soul. He had to get to her.

Terror painted the sky and red-painted the ground. Death was upon them, and the smell of it was suffocating.

There was a short reprieve of gunfire as Greg was battling Penelope for control of her gun. Then everything happened at once. Archie and Shalamar were able to get to Theory and take the children while he focused on getting to Virtuous.

It felt as if they were continents apart, but nothing was stopping him from getting to her. He screamed out her name, telling her to hold on. She did not reply nor did her body react to acknowledge his voice. His mind went to the last text he sent, a Bible verse, and in response, she sent him a prayer. He wondered would that be it; was today all they had? "God please don't take her from me. I beg you, Father, don't take her," he whispered as he quickened his pace to get to her.

More gunshots ensued; panic should have captured him, but his love for Virtuous powered him on. Her need for him was his motivation. At that moment, as frightened as he was for her life, he felt invincible. God would not have brought them this far to leave them. His only thought was of her.

Theory quickly dropped to his knees and pulled Virtuous' limp body to him. She was losing blood; her light skin began to pale, and tears unknowingly slipped down his face. It was not supposed to happen like this. They had hope and a future. He still owed her the best of memories. There was so much for them to do; jealousy and obsession would not be the ending of their love story. It was just beginning; life with her was just beginning, he would not lose her.

"Baby, hold you. Please hold on. Forever and always, Proverbs." he whispered.

A & Ω

"Selma getting out the hospital next year?" Nocturnal asked Staci as she assisted Quinton in helping him get adjusted in the wheelchair. They had just finished his noon workout, and Quinton was helping him to get set up for lunch. Since the change in attitude, he was performing at a level that had his doctors mystified. Attitude really was everything. He was thankful for getting himself together.

"Yeah. She'll probably have some mental and physical delays and will rely on us for the rest of her life. Our daughter is strong, and she is pulling through. Little-by-little, she's meeting her milestones. She's also gained some weight."

Nocturnal nodded, a small smile graced his face at Staci's update. He had not physically seen his daughter since his accident, and he missed her. Staci and his mom were taking loads of pictures and sharing them with him. Hearing that she was improving was promising.

There was something else on his mind that he wanted to address. He was waiting for Quinton to finish up and leave first, though.

"Do you need anything else?" Quinton asked.

"Nah, I'm good. Thanks."

Quinton nodded and exited the room shutting the door behind him.

"Staci, I've been meaning to ask you about Jedidiah."

Staci looked up from her book and glanced at him. "What about him?"

The look on her face gave nothing away. Since talking to Mama Kabila and working with the pastor at Staci's church, he wanted to be the best parent to his daughter. Also, he wanted Staci to know though her actions hurt him, he still cared about her wellbeing. He wanted to make sure that she was making the right decisions.

"Y'all dating?"

Staci laughed a soulful, cleansing laugh. Nocturnal was unsure what to make of her reaction. Their relationship had been on edge, but after his sister attacked Staci, he was doing his best to let go of the past.

"Are you dating Lourdes?"

It was like that? She was going to answer a question by asking one. "Nah, it ain't like that with her. I did apologize to her for how I treated her. I'm a father of two daughters, and I would never want a man to treat Sadie or Selma like that. Seriously, I'm just trying to get straight, so I can deal with these charges. I'm thankful they're holding off since I'm so messed up, letting me bail out. Between Mama Kabila and my attorney, I think I'm going to be good. Hopefully, the DA will drop all the charges or let me off on probation."

Staci nodded as she sat down and powered on the television.

"So, I should be released in a few weeks, probably going to miss Christmas and New Year's. They're discharging me to a rehab facility, and then I'll learn how to walk with my prosthetic."

"That's good news. Fingers crossed our daughter will be discharged soon as well. We'll throw a party for both of you."

"Yeah," Nocturnal replied. Then he added, "Staci, I'm sorry."

He watched as her body stiffened at his apology. Probably because she had never heard him say those words and mean them. He was sorry. Being in his current predicament that has altered his life significantly gave him a lot of alone time to contemplate.

Staci's dark eyes roved in his direction. They were watery. It was as if everything that she had been carrying was finally lifting off her shoulders. He could see the variety of emotions that etched her face. Then she closed her eyes and inhaled deeply, almost as if a prayer had been answered.

Nocturnal recognized that he had put her through unnecessary misery because of his selfish actions. It was time to accept responsibility and do better for himself and his family.

"I'm sorry, too. I just pray that from this moment on, we co-parent our children and do our best to work together, even though we aren't together."

Before Nocturnal could reply, his landline rang. The only people who called to the room were his mom or sister. He hadn't spoken to Penelope since she lost it on Staci. From speaking to his mom, Penelope was not taking the breakup well. As promised, Big EZ sent her divorce papers.

Without a second thought, he answered the phone.

"Yo."

"Percy, it's Sharifa. Is Staci there with you?"

"Yeah. You wanna speak to her."

"In a minute, but I need you to listen to me. Your sister did something horrible this morning, and a lot of innocent people got hurt."

"What? I mean what my sister do now?" he asked half-heartedly, rolling his eyes in frustration.

There was silence on the other end; it was so long that Nocturnal thought Sharifa had hung up on him.

"Hello?"

"She attempted to murder Big EZ's kids, all of them."

Nocturnal's entire body went stiff. There was no way she said what he thought she said. Penelope was not that stupid. "Hol' up. Where's Evie and Evan?"

At that, Staci dropped the remote and glared at Nocturnal, waiting to be informed about what was going on.

"In the hospital, scared but alive. She tried to smother them to death, so they pretended to be dead. It's like she just lost her mind. Then she went down to the ice rink to kill the twins. It's all over the local news. Like, real-time; every news channel is reporting on it. Oh lord, from what I heard it was horrible. The kids were there. I'm talking about Sadie, Chauncory, and other children. They say she just started shooting."

Nocturnal's entire body shook. "No, no, no, is anybody dead? Tell me, did she hurt my kids? This karma times a hundred." He wept.

"What? Who hurt our kids!" Staci screeched. Her dark eyes turned watery. She quickly picked up her cell phone and attempted to call Theory. It was then that she saw she had missed at least a dozen calls.

She had left her phone in the room and hadn't thought about it until just now.

"I don't know for sure. I'm just trying to get to the hospital. Tell Staci, please. I called her several times, but she hasn't answered or called back. I'll keep you updated as I find out more."

"Okay," was all he could muster after hearing the devastating news.

Nocturnal shook his head in disbelief. Why would Penelope do something so asinine and selfish? He closed his eyes and let a tear fall.

"What's going on?!" Staci bellowed.

"My sister really lost it. She went on a rampage, trying to kill all of Big EZ's kids, including her own, just to get back at him. I ain't never thought my sister was capable of something so diabolical. Ever."

Staci shook her head in disbelief. She knew that Penelope was off. She knew that Penelope could hurt anyone she thought would harm her relationship with EZ. How could she hurt her own children? "Did she hurt our children, too?"

"Your mama said she don't know. We need to find out what's going on. I swear, ain't no man worth losing your life or taking a life. I, mean, how could she stoop so low?"

Staci was a ball of nerves, and she called everyone associated with Theory. "I should have spoken up sooner. Now, the blood on her hands are on mine, too, and I put everyone had risk," Staci tearfully mourned. "I can't lose our children. I can't."

"Shush, Staci, they're fine. You hear me? They're fine."

CHAPTER 23

Theory's gait was smooth, not at all showcasing the burning fury that was seeping from his heart to the rest of his body. Sleepless nights had assailed him; the soft whimpers of his children had brought him to his knees. He prayed harder over the last week than he ever had in his entire life. Chauncory and Tory would only sleep if they were in bed with him, and they demanded to see Virtuous. Every part of his fiber wanted to erase the trauma the children faced when Penelope decided to take her revenge out on Big EZ.

Guilt ate away at Theory for not seeing it sooner. Penelope was just as much of a threat as Greg, but that insight had come almost too late. Several families and countless lives had been altered because of jealousy, obsession, and revenge. Innocent children were hurt as they sought safety from the gunfire.

Now, it would end.

Smiling at the nurse's assistant, Theory made a quick right and dapped down the hall to a room that was supposedly off-limits to him. He had a friend in Montez, so he entered Greg's hospital room.

"Nurse?" the raspy voice called out, his blue eyes staring out the window. He was pitiful now.

Theory did not speak as he gaited closer to the man he had only seen through Virtuous' eyes. A man that had tormented the woman that he loved but also gave him the greatest gift now that he had Tory.

"Nurse?" Greg asked again, only this time, he slowly turned his head. His eyes widened at the sight before him. "You."

It was one word, but it was accusatory and violent. Theory was unmovable. They needed to have a conversation and once they did, Greg would become invisible. He would enter the realm of nothingness to him. Theory needed Greg to know that his plan to ruin the beautiful light that was Virtuous Atarah All failed. Addison failed and so did Penelope. His baby's light was going to shine no matter what.

"It's me, Greg. Finally, we meet. I haven't seen you since I first met Virtuous in Gaffney," Theory replied coolly as he pulled up a chair to nearer to Greg. How times change. The arrogant smug look that Virtuous had described was no longer there. His invincibility had met its match. Greg was now paralyzed from the waist down.

Greg cut his eyes at Theory, turning his nose up. A smirk formed on his face. "You think you've won, don't you? This is just a temporary setback. You can't have my family," Greg boasted.

Theory inhaled a deep breath and slowly exhaled it, holding Greg's gaze. "Correction, you can't have my family.

Greg's eyes twitched at the surety of the young man. Then his face balled up in anger before smoothing out again. "I had her first. She'll always be mine. I'm in her mind," Greg countered.

Theory chuckled and threw his head back. The old him, the unsaved him, would have put hands on Greg at what he was insinuating; however, he was no longer that man. He'd been transformed. Where he was once led in the flesh, he was now led by the spirit.

"Greg, you took from Virtuous. You had her fear, but I give to Virtuous, my Proverbs. In turn, she gives to me. I earned her love and affection.

"You may have touched her first, but your touch was violent and unwanted. I touch the parts of her that you never have. I'm her last and forever. See, you mishandled a gift God gave to you, but I treasure her daily. I treasure who she is, what she's overcome, and the mother she is to *our* daughter and son. What you meant to do was destroy who God created her to be so that you could remake her in your image. That's not how it works. You are simply a man. God is God. He can't be beaten; victory is always His.

"You lose. God promised her hope and a future, and I promised her better memories. God doesn't lie, and neither do I. What happened to you is not a temporary setback; it's God."

Greg stared at him, but there was no remorse in his eyes, though Theory knew he heard all that was said. He did not seem like a man who learned anything easy. He was going to have a tough road ahead of him. That was no longer Theory's concern.

Theory pushed the chair back and was making his exodus from the room when Greg spoke.

"I'm Tory's father. I always will be, and that connects me to Virtue. I love her. I saved her!" he attempted to shout. It came out in a pitiful whimper.

Theory turned around and shook his head. Dude was next-level sick. "Nah, what you did to Virtuous was never about love. Let me drop some knowledge on you. Matthew 18:6 states, *Whoever causes one of these little ones who believe in Me to sin, it would be better for him if a millstone were hung around his neck, and he were drowned in the depth of the sea.* You got bigger problems, and I suggest you get to repenting and praying. Judgment day is coming, and it's not looking good for you."

Theory turned to leave but stopped again and gave Greg one last glance. "We forgive you. I spoke to Virtuous and the kids, and collectively, we've decided to forgive you. We don't absolve you, but our love for God is stronger than anything. You've taken enough from my girl and *my* daughter. They aren't yours anymore. You're like the man in the Bible who buried his talents. God gave them to the man with ten talents, and that's me. Enjoy the mess you created."

That sent Greg into a fitful rage, and Theory left him just like that.

A & Ω

"I'm okay, Daddy, and so is Valor. He didn't even get shot," Virtuous reassured her father. He was beating himself up about what Penelope had attempted to do. Sadly, she had come to take lives, but it was she who ended up dead. That broke Virtuous' heart. Now her sister and brother had to know what it was like to be motherless. It was selfish and unfathomable what Penelope did. Today, she was being buried. Virtuous wondered if anyone would attend the funeral.

"You were shot."

"I know. According to Archie, I can officially become a gangster rapper," she teased.

"Virtuous," he warned.

"Sorry, it was just a joke. I'm alive. Let's focus on that."

He sighed. "You're too good, Virtuous."

She smiled, even though he could not see it. "It would be counterproductive to live in anger. Besides, I have kids and my siblings to be concerned about. I can't live in a negative space. Everyone has been amazing, and their prayers are what has kept us all together. You need to stay positive and finish out these last few months so we can be a family."

"I love you, girl. You got that good heart like your mama. I'll be cool. They're releasing you today?"

"Yes. GG and Papaw Hartford are fussing over where I'm going to stay once I'm released. GG wants me to spend winter break with her."

Big EZ laughed. "My mama gonna get what she wants. Hey, is Valor with you?"

"Yes, I'll pass him the phone." Just as Virtuous handed her brother the phone, her hospital door opened, and Theory entered.

He looked handsome as always. A sweet grin etched across her face. His was the voice she held onto after being shot. It was his scent that kept her in the present. Theory saved her life.

"Hey, baby," she greeted as he entered. Tory was napping on the bed. Theory's eyes went to Tory and then back to her. He sauntered over and kissed her cheek sweetly.

He lovingly ran his fingers down her face before saying, "The nurse is coming with your discharge papers. I figure I'll take you to Grammy's. Chauncory wants to see you before he heads to Atlanta to spend time with his mama and them."

"Good; I'm ready to go home. Daddy called while you were gone."

"Yeah, is that who Val is talking to?"

Theory smiled.

A & Ω

Nocturnal felt more broken now than he felt when he found out he was missing his leg. Penelope was not the person he thought she was. Words could not express how he felt. There was nothing he could say or do to heal the brokenness that Penelope left behind.

Her action shattered lives. His mother mourned, and Mama Kabila was right by her side because she knew the pain of losing a child although under very different circumstances. It wasn't the same. Congo's life was taken by accident; his sister intended to take the lives of four innocent children and then her own.

She made her family feel guilty for grieving her loss. Guilty because her actions could have eliminated children who had done nothing more but be born and live. Guilty because she had already taken a life because she feared competition. Guilty because she left her mother and brother to clean up her mess. Letting out a shaky breath, Nocturnal allowed the tears to fall.

Never did he think their lives would turn out like this.

Evonne and Evan had lost a mother, a mother that attempted to kill them. How had it come to this? That was a question that would remain unanswered because she was gone now. She left a letter behind stating she was going to kill the kids and then herself. She wanted to hurt Big EZ as he hurt her. Her logic and actions were erratic and flawed. Killing those kids wouldn't have just hurt their father, but it would have crushed several families. She would have accomplished nothing.

It was her life that had been taken, and it was she who was now being buried. Nocturnal could not be there due to his injuries. He didn't know if his mother had even attended. The funeral had to be kept a secret due to the anger and outrage of Penelope's actions. It was all over the news and social media. Penelope was despised. His family was hated and part of him understood. How many lives had his actions taken? Yeah, his family was a bunch of murderers and attempted murderers. What really bothered Nocturnal was that he had no idea if his sister was in Heaven or Hell. That uncertainty was what finally changed his life.

It burned his soul that her soul might not be safe. On this day, one life ended a new one would begin. He was giving his life to God.

Nocturnal witnessed what being without God could do, and he didn't want to continue a life that did not have God as the leader. He only followed himself, and that cost him his best friend, almost a child, and his independence. He was hearing God. He was a goon, but now, he was going to be a child of God.

Nocturnal reached for his new cell phone and dialed Theory.

"Yo."

"Man, it's Noc. Can we talk?"

"Yeah, what's up?"

"I'm ready. I'm ready for Jesus. No more street, no more doing me, so can you help me?"

"Absolutely."

CHAPTER 24

2016

"Dadeee," Tory's sweet voice crooned. She was running as fast as her little legs could go. Behind her were Logic and Chauncory. The innocence of the moment choked him up momentarily. Their happiness was what kept him going. It had been a rough four months.

All Theory wanted to do was protect the children. At least now, Greg was in prison awaiting trial. Addison was serving time after getting a plea deal, but Mamaw LeAnn was still in denial.

Virtuous and Theory decided it was best to keep Tory away from her until things were more settled. Maddison was in the custody of Cate and Norman. Tommy Leigh, the father of Addison and Valerie had attempted to gain custody but lost the custody case. Now, things were calmer.

"Get me, Dada!" Tory yelled and Theory quickly scooped her up in his arms and smothered her with kisses. He made sure to put in extra time with the kids. He knew firsthand what untreated trauma could do. They were all currently seeing Serena.

"Daddy, Grammy said it's time to go. Tory's not supposed to be running in her new dress," Chauncory reminded.

Theory laughed at the seriousness of his son. He did not slack off when it came to his big brother duties.

"You're right, son. We have to look nice for Virtuous' senior art show," Theory agreed as he fixed his son's bowtie. "You're looking sharp."

Chauncory smiled brightly. "Thanks, Daddy. C'mon, Grammy said they're serving chocolate cupcakes."

Theory snickered. "Alright, let's go root Proverbs on."

A & Ω

Joy and nerves. Yes, that described Virtuous perfectly. Today was a big day for her and her family. There was life after a tragedy.

Virtuous had taken two bullets—one to her ankle, which shattered it, and one to her leg. She now walked with a limp, but Theory said it added to her beauty.

For her, it was a reminder of the goodness of God. That day, she could have died, or if Greg had his way, she could have been kidnapped and living in hiding. However, God saw fit to allow her more time. For that, she was thankful.

Now, she was finally showcasing her artwork. After everything that happened, she needed an outlet for it all. This show was not just to show her talent but to also show that she was a survivor and that God could use anyone at any time to be a blessing. God used a young man, abandoned and neglected, sold for drugs, to show Virtuous she had worth.

Her show consisted of three stages, a metamorphosis of her life. Each stage had been emotional to paint and draw. She had used a variety of techniques.

In the back of her mind, the sermon KILL BILL was still prevalent, and her artwork showcased that. A girl who was stuck in bondage, surrounded by insecurity, and believed in lies and felt such deep loneliness had risen from the ashes again and again.

"*All of me*, are you ready? I got you something." The voice with the honeyed bass rippled through her thoughts.

Virtuous knew exactly who that was. Her dad had his own special name for her; it was 'All of me'. That made her feel special. Finally, she had a father.

A smile broadened on her face as she turned slowly around to see him. Ezekiel All was one of her most favorite people. The fact that he had the Marketside Chocolate Turtle Brownie cookies gave her life. "Daddy, I need that sugar. Do you have a Cheerwine to go with it?" That was something she recently started to like.

Ezekiel winked and replied, "Of course. Daddy is on his A-game tonight. My baby is a superstar. Vincent van Gogh and *The Starry Night* got nothing on you."

Virtuous could only grin at his enthusiasm. He handed her the drink and one cookie. She was eighteen, but he measured out her sugar as if she was eight. Though there was a smile on his face, his eyes still held sorrow and guilt. He blamed himself for what Penelope had done, first to Valerie and then what she attempted to do to his children.

Penelope was a special kind of crazy, but also, somewhere deep inside, she had to be lonely and full of fear. Something just broke in her. That was because she placed her faith in a man and not in God. People must be careful or what they love becomes an obsession, an idol, and that kills.

"It's okay, Daddy. We're still a family. You finally have all your children together and a beautiful granddaughter that thinks the world of you. Guilt no longer has a place in your heart. Only love, Daddy; just love."

Big EZ took a deep breath before pulling Virtuous into his chest and kissing the top of her head. "My mind and heart just can't let it go. That woman took the love of my life and then tried to take all my children from me. One day, it'll be okay, but today isn't it. I wish my heart was as open and as forgiving as yours. I'm so grateful for you. The way you view life is astounding. I love that about you, baby girl. You're all of me."

Virtuous inhaled her father's scent. It was so much better seeing him out of prison. "I love you, Daddy. I believe with all my heart that God will remove the guilt and the pain."

"Amen. I'm going to let you finish getting ready. Just know that we, all your sisters and brothers, even the two that aren't mine, are extremely proud of you."

He was talking about Jason and Maddison. For some reason, Jason really seemed taken with Ezekiel, and her father treated him no differently than he treated her. He kissed her once more and then left, leaving her alone. Virtuous took the moment to pray and praise God.

A & Ω

"Good evening, everyone. Thank you all so much for coming out to support my senior project. Most of my artwork will be available for purchase. A portion of all sales will be donated to various organizations that work with domestic violence and sexual assault survivors." Virtuous took a deep breath and looked to her left where Theory stood. He nodded his head in encouragement. He had heard this speech before and assured her that she could do it. "As you all may or may not know, I'm a survivor of physical and sexual abuse, and my artwork showcases my life at its worst and at its best. It's a representation of what God has done. God uses those who others overlook as His vessels so that we all remember that God can use anyone to be a blessing and to restore hope to the hopeless. That's my mission tonight. As you view the pieces that I've painted, remember life isn't about wealth, intelligence, race, or gender. It's about having the heart to love, to serve, and to allow God you use you as He sees fit. The Theory of All, which is the title of my showcase, is about trusting God so much that even in the darkest of darkness the light of hope lingers. Just one flick of the flame and your life will change."

The claps and whistles started. Virtuous knew it was her Dad. He was so extra, but that was okay. These were the moments she wished for and now she had them, a real family, a good man that loved her and her daughter, and peace of mind. God said He knows the plans he has, plans of peace and not of evil, to give a future and a hope. With Addison, Greg, and Penelope out of her life, her future was looking brighter. Inside of her pocket were several college acceptance letters. It was time to live and live she would.

EPILOGUE

Theory ran the lint brush over Deacon Hayes' linen suit. Today was a big day for him as well for Stanley. They were having a double wedding ceremony. Apparently, Stanley and Ms. Willamina were having a lowkey romance. Through Nocturnal, he found out the two were dating, which was fine with him as long as Ms. Willamina was good to Cordy. He loved his little sister and would not allow anyone, Stanley included, to mistreat her.

So much had changed over the summer. He and Virtuous were both going to attend school in North Carolina. He finally met his maternal grandparents, and they got along well. He had to check his cousin for flirting with Virtuous, but once he hemmed him up, everything went smoothly.

"How do I look?"

"You look good. Grammy is going to swoon over you," Theory teased, causing Deacon Hayes to laugh."

"What's so funny?" Stanley asked, followed by his five brothers and Valor. Valor was Deacon Hayes' best man.

"Nothing, just teasing the groom."

Stanley nodded. Theory could sense by his eyes that he wanted to talk to him.

Stanley cleared his throat and asked if he could have the room. Everyone exited except for Valor. The two were always close, but after the shooting, Valor was even more protective of his family. Theory nodded to let him know it was cool.

Stanley turned but remained silent. Theory figured he understood.

"Thank you for being my best man. I know I was never the best father, but I see that you've learned from my mistakes. You're wonderful with Chauncory and Tory. They look at you like you're a superhero."

Theory nodded. This was Stanley's moment, and he was not going to interrupt. A lot had happened after their epic fight. Theory was man enough to let go of the anger and the hurt. He needed to get his feelings out and now that he had, he was good.

Stanley sighed. "I love you, Theory. I'm so sorry about how I treated you. Don't ever think that you did anything wrong. You were the only good thing I did in life. Had I not given my soul to drugs—" he stopped. That was when Theory noticed that he was crying. For the first time, his father's tears affected him.

Without a thought, he pulled his father into a hug. "Let it go. You did wrong; now you're doing right. You've found yourself a good woman who loves you and Cordy. You got a good job; you're clean, and you're moving forward in life. That's a blessing. Don't worry about what was. I'm good. There's no anger in me toward you. Be happy." Stanley held him a little tighter and then let him go.

"Thank you. You think we'll ever get that father/son bond?"

"Only God knows. C'mon before your future wife thinks you've left her at the altar. You know them Anderson homies, including Nocturnal with his bionic leg, will cut a fool."

Stanley burst out laughing. "This is good, us talking like this."

"It is. Let's keep talking and see what happens. I do appreciate all the help you gave me when I thought I was going to lose Proverbs. That meant a lot to me."

"That's what a father does. You have my word that while breath is in my body, I'll have your back.

Theory smiled. "Thanks."

A & Ω

Later that night, everyone was dancing. Nocturnal shook his head to the beat. Sadie was sitting on his lap, taking a break. She and Tory were instant best friends and had been running the entire yard with Theory's dog Logic.

"Daddy, can I go get a cupcake? Auntie Vivi just brought out some more." Nocturnal did a quick scan. He didn't see Staci, so he told her yes and requested she bring him one as well. Staci had said no more sugar, but he could not tell his baby girl no. At least this way, they would go down together.

Leaning back in his chair, he let out a soft chuckle. Who would have ever thought he would be here like this? A man he thought his enemy was now counted as a friend. His daughter called Theory uncle, and Virtuous aunt. Theory's daughter called him Uncle Noc and Staci, aunt. For the life of Nocturnal, he could not remember why he was so threatened by Theory. He was a good dude. They were family now, linked together through Chauncory and Virtuous and Valor. Man, he wished Congo could see this. He missed his best friend daily, but they would be reunited again. He believed that.

It still shocked him sometimes, but tragedy can sometimes bring clarity.

He was sure that God had a sense of humor because Nocturnal would have never seen this coming. He liked it; nah he loved it.

"Noc, are we dancing or what?" Staci asked, bringing him back to the present. Before he could speak, Archie popped up.

"Look, before you get to dancing, is that million-dollar leg insured? Don't nobody got the money to be replacing that leg. All I can do is chop down a tree and peg leg that bad boy."

Staci howled in laughter. "Archie, why, though? You always messin' wit somebody. You're forever teasing him about his leg."

"What? Theo says he family, so I'm just treating him like everybody else. No wobbling for you, just stick to two-stepping. If that leg comes off and hit me, we're fighting."

Nocturnal shook his head. Archie was a special kind of different. He could not even be offended. It was just Archie.

"For real, though, I'll tell Trek to put on some slow jams. We follow ADA guidelines."

"ADA guidelines?" Nocturnal asked.

"Man, yeah; Americans with Disabilities Act."

"You stupid, Archie; leave me alone and go get your girl. Look like my son over there making moves."

Archie turned and shook his head. "Ain't it his bedtime? He got two sets of parents, and ain't not a one of you checking him. That's what wrong with America now. Treating your children like farmers do their chickens and let them free range. Don't make no sense. He over there trying to Luther Vandross my girl. It be your own nephew doing you dirty," he fussed before marching off.

Both Staci and Nocturnal laughed at his antics.

"Are we dancing?"

"Well, I was waiting for baby girl to bring me a cupcake."

"Your daughter ate her cupcake and yours, too. She over there with my mama about ready to pass out from a sugar overdose."

"Well, let's two-step."

The two walked to the dance floor and began to dance. This was another blessing that Noc had not seen coming. Staci took him back. The authorities put him on probation and once that happened, Nocturnal confessed his love for Staci. He wanted to be a family man. He desired to raise their children together, and he wanted Staci by his side. They relocated to Atlanta. The pair had joint custody of Chauncory.

Chauncory was moving to North Carolina with Virtuous and Theory but would spend his summers in Georgia with Noc and Staci. Either party could visit at any time. There was nothing but love and respect between the families.

After what Penelope did, Nocturnal thought that Big EZ, his children, and Theory would hate him. Instead. they embraced him. Their actions were nurturing his walk with Christ. He was a better man, father, and soon-to-be husband because of them.

"I love you, Staci. Thank you for giving me another chance at being a better man."

Staci smiled.

"I love you, too. We're doing it right this time. I'm all in. No lies, no regrets, just love."

"Yeah, baby, just love."

A & Ω

"Theo, come get ya son. He over here spitting game to my girl. Out here singing Sweet Lady lyrics like he's Tyrese, showing all them white baby teeth, knowing he done lost two. Done graduated from kindergarten and think he Casanova. It's his bedtime, bruh," Archie fussed, causing Theory to bend over in laughter.

"Archie, don't do your nephew like that. He doesn't mean any harm."

"No harm? I can't tell it."

"He's just having fun," Shalamar teased.

Archie laughed good-naturedly. "For real, it's past his bedtime. All of these kids running on sugar fumes."

"Let me go 'round up my kid crew and get them to bed. I'll come holla at y'all later."

Theory took off to get Chauncory, and then the pair ambled over to Virtuous who was holding a sleeping Tory. She was surrounded by

Tamari, Maisha, and Rika. Theory was happy at how the Mai and Rika and become fast friends with Virtuous and Tamari.

"Babe, I was taking this one to bed and figured Tory was ready for bed, too."

Virtuous nodded in agreement. She told her friends she would be back as she followed Theory into the house. As a team, they quickly got the kids undressed, washed, and dressed again before putting them into bed.

One hour later, Virtuous and Theory were sitting together, enjoying the scenery around them. Grammy hadn't stopped dancing yet. There was a joy in her eyes that Theory had not seen since his grandfather died. Then there was Stanley; the man looked alive. Ms. Willamina looked like she had something to live for. She and Stanley were preparing for Nora Jean to give birth so they could raise Congo's child together.

Theory was in awe at how God worked that out. It was so beautiful how something wonderful blossomed out of tragedy.

Now, he finally had Virtuous. He was worry-free. There was no Greg to worry about. Addison was no longer an issue. Theory let out the biggest breath he could then he pulled Virtuous closer to him and kissed her.

"One day soon, I hope this will be us. We'll be celebrating our marriage and then Tory will officially be a Campbell."

Virtuous smiled. "I never thought it could be like this. I don't always understand why God allows things to happen the way He does, but I'm thankful. With all my talent, I could've never painted this. I thank God every night for you." She turned and smiled at Theory. "I love Theory Campbell. I had no idea when I met you that day at the outlet that my life would change for the better. You're beyond anything I could ever imagine or pray for."

"I love you, always and forever, Proverbs. You're my virtuous woman."

THE END!

Y. Deonna's Book List & Contact Info
Book Catalog

Deception Has A Name (rerelease)
Her Mistake, His Masterpiece (rerelease)
Healing A Bitter Heart (Formally Bitter Root 1 & 2)
Battle Scarred Love 1 BWWM (This Kind of Love)
Battle Scarred Love 2
The Virtuous Trilogy

Connect:
Email: authorydeonna@gmail.com
Join the new Facebook group to be in the know
IG: bluetygrezz
Twitter: @CrownedRuby
Facebook page: fb.me/Authorydeonna
Join the mailing list

www.ingramcontent.com/pod-product-compliance
Lightning Source LLC
Chambersburg PA
CBHW052134170626
46812CB00004B/1404